Oh Lord, I do

He'd seen several ⸻ life, but it never got an ⸻ urn her over.

She groaned, causing him to jump back in surprise.

As the morning sun touched her features, he detected a faint blush of pink staining her pale cheeks and full lips. This was no dead body!

Heart pounding, he dropped to his knees beside the woman. Taking her cool hands into his, he began rubbing warmth into her long, delicate fingers.

Her eyelids, fringed by thick dark lashes, fluttered open.

Slipping his left arm beneath her back, Jacob lifted her head and upper torso from the riverbank. "It's all right. You're going to be all right," he assured her, brushing hair and sand from her face with his free hand.

Her lips parted to emit another soft groan.

Jacob wrenched his attention from the arresting beauty of the woman to focus upon her plight. "You'll be all right now," he repeated. "I'm going to take care of you."

RAMONA K. CECIL is a wife, mother, grandmother, freelance poet, and award-winning inspirational romance writer. Now empty nesters, she and her husband make their home in Indiana. She's a member of American Christian Fiction Writers and American Christian Fiction Writers Indiana Chapter, and her work has won awards in a number of inspirational writing contests. Over eighty of her inspirational verses have been published on a wide array of items for the Christian gift market. She enjoys a speaking ministry, sharing her journey to publication while encouraging aspiring writers. When not writing, her hobbies include reading, gardening, and visiting places of historical interest.

Sweet
Forever

Ramona K. Cecil

Heartsong Presents

"There's a land beyond the river,
That we call the sweet forever—"
from *When They Ring Those Golden Bells*
by Daniel de Marbelle

Special thanks to the local history and genealogy department of the Madison Jefferson County Public Library; Historic Madison, Inc., Madison, Indiana; Jefferson County Historical Society; Verdin Company and the Verdin Bell and Clock Museum of Cincinnati, Ohio; Kim Sawyer and Staci Wilder for their invaluable critique work on this project; and my husband, Jim, and daughters, Jennifer and Kelly, whose encouragement and support make what I do possible.

A note from the Author:
I love to hear from my readers! You may correspond with me by writing:

Ramona K. Cecil
Author Relations
PO Box 721
Uhrichsville, OH 44683

ISBN 978-1-60260-009-6

SWEET FOREVER

All scripture quotations are taken from the King James Version of the Bible.

All of the characters and events in this book are fictitious. Any resemblance to actual persons, living or dead, or to actual events is purely coincidental.

Our mission is to publish and distribute inspirational products offering exceptional value and biblical encouragement to the masses.

PRINTED IN THE U.S.A.

one

Ohio River at Madison, Indiana, April 1845

Tap, tap, tap.

Rosaleen Archer fixed her attention on the silver tip of Bill McGurty's walking stick.

Tap, tap, tap.

Its hypnotic cadence against the floor of her riverboat cabin held her in a terrified trance.

"You'll be a good girl this evening, won't you, Rosaleen?" The corner of his black clipped mustache twisted in a tiny sneer.

Rosaleen nodded, swallowing hard past the wad of fear in her throat.

"There's my good girl." The reflection of the wall sconce taper's flame danced in his small black eyes. "I'd hate to have to punish you again."

Tap, tap, tap.

He reached his hand out toward her, and Rosaleen moved away, pressing her back against the cabin wall. Shivering, she turned her face from the cold touch of his fingers on her cheek.

"You know what to do." The silky sweetness left his voice as he glanced at his silver watch then slipped it back into the pocket of his scarlet brocade vest "Wait about an hour, till we're well into the game and they're well into their cups, then you can join us."

Again she nodded. Anything to make him leave her alone.

He pinched her chin hard between his forefinger and thumb.

Rosaleen fought nausea as he pressed a whiskey-laden kiss on her lips.

"Make me some money tonight." He lifted his dark beaver

hat from the wrought iron hook beside the door to the Grand Saloon. With a parting wink, he set the hat at a jaunty angle atop his slicked-down black hair.

Long moments after her cabin door closed, Rosaleen sat trembling on the little bunk affixed to one wall of the cramped room. She looked around the dimly lit, whitewashed cabin that was, for all practical purposes, her prison cell. The bunk and a tiny washstand against the opposite wall were the only comforts afforded by the five-by-six-foot area.

Tonight marked exactly six months since her husband's death aboard the steamboat *River Queen*. Shivering, she relived the sight of Bill McGurty accusing Donovan of cheating at cards. She'd watched Bill pull out the wicked little derringer, heard the shot, and saw Donovan jerk back then fall forward.

As awful as that sight had been, what followed eclipsed it in terror. Bill McGurty declared the act self-defense since Donovan also carried a derringer. No one at the table dared dispute his claim. Pronouncing himself Rosaleen's "protector," he quickly became the opposite, forcing her to move with him from riverboat to riverboat.

For Rosaleen, the months since had amounted to a swift descent into a horrible existence. The shame of how Bill had used her night after night burned inside her like a spirit-consuming flame.

I'll die before I let him touch me again.

In an act of defiance, she snatched her little black velvet reticule from the beside table, fished out the gold ring Donovan had placed on her hand eight months ago, and slipped it back on her finger. She would leave the cabin tonight—but not to help Black Jack Bill McGurty. Her plan of escape had begun when they'd boarded the *Cortland Belle* two days ago in Cincinnati and she'd learned Arthur Ellis piloted the boat.

During their short marriage, Donovan had mentioned Mr. Ellis, a fellow riverboat pilot, as a friend. If she could only manage a moment alone with him, perhaps he'd protect her and make Bill answer for his crimes when they docked at Louisville, Kentucky. Somehow she must make her way to the pilot's cabin on the Texas deck at the top of the boat.

Rosaleen glanced at the two doors on either side of her cabin. One led to the outer deck, the other to the Grand Saloon. Their first night on the *Cortland Belle*, she'd attempted an escape through the door to the outer deck. But a couple of Bill's gambling cronies had caught her on the promenade deck and returned her to her captor. She pressed her fingers against her ribs, still sore from the beating the thwarted attempt had elicited. Tonight she would try again. But this time she had a different strategy in mind.

It had been no more than a half hour, she guessed, since Bill had left her cabin. Yet if she waited longer, he would be expecting her to appear beside him at the gambling tables. Gathering her courage along with the purple silk folds of her skirts, she stood and walked to the door that opened to the Grand Saloon.

The beginnings of a prayer withered inside her as the scowling visage of her former guardian assembled itself in her mind. Reverend Wilfred Maguire, the elder brother of her late adoptive father, had made it quite clear—because of her illegitimacy God wanted nothing to do with her.

She must depend upon the gambler's luck of Rory Maguire, the man who'd raised her as his own and who in her heart would always be "Papa."

All that's required is but a little smile from Lady Luck.

Remembering her father's frequent maxim, Rosaleen hoped Lady Luck would beam tonight.

She touched her mother's brooch pinned to the bodice of her dress. A gift from her father on her tenth birthday, the bejeweled cameo had always helped Rosaleen feel closer to the mother she'd never known. . .and the adoptive father she still missed.

Rosaleen blinked back hot tears. *Oh Papa, how I wish you were here to help me.*

The strong odors of cigar smoke and whiskey assailed her nostrils as she entered the Grand Saloon. A lively banjo tune blended with the cacophony of conversation and hearty laughter.

A Persian carpet of maroon, gold, and blue covered the entire floor area, stretching over two hundred feet long and nearly twenty feet wide. A row of brass and crystal chandeliers hanging along the center of the ceiling lit the opulent expanse. Rosaleen thought the saloon, richly decorated with silk upholstered chairs, horsehair sofas, and ornately carved marble-topped tables, one of the nicer ones she'd seen during her life aboard the steamboats.

As she moved along the wall of cabin doors, her heart pounded. She shot quick glances across the room where Bill sat laughing at a gambling table, chewing on an unlit cigar. Perhaps Lady Luck would continue smiling and Bill would not notice her.

"Rosaleen!"

Her heart dropped. Managing a shaky smile, she made her way toward Bill McGurty and the half dozen other men around the table.

"A bit early, ain't ya?" Bill's smile never reached his black eyes.

"Sorry." She remembered the sting of his ebony walking stick against her back, and a cold shiver slithered through her.

"Here's a V-spot. Be a good girl and go get us another couple of bottles of whiskey from the bar." He tucked the five-dollar note into the bodice of her dress.

Rosaleen nodded, realizing Lady Luck had just begun smiling like crazy. The bar was at the front end of the Grand Saloon, next to the door that led to the outer deck. With just a bit more luck she might be able to steal away without Bill's seeing her.

Just a few more steps.

When she slipped through the door, a fresh breeze welcomed her at the outside promenade of mid-deck. She rubbed her bare arms in the chill night air of early spring.

With a nervous glance over her shoulder at the door to the Grand Saloon, Rosaleen stepped toward the short stairway to the Texas deck. There, just below the pilothouse, were the cabins of the crew, including that of pilot Arthur Ellis. Pausing at the bottom step, she rehearsed the petition she would present to her late husband's friend.

Suddenly, the night exploded in a deafening flash of orange and yellow. The deck bucked like an unbroken colt, sending her flying against the rail.

Bruised and stunned, Rosaleen pulled herself up by the rail. In shock, she looked around at her altered surroundings. The pilothouse and much of the steamboat's stern no longer existed. All her life, she'd heard horror stories of boiler explosions. *Is that what just happened?*

Fire engulfed the back half of the boat. Its hungry crackle mixed with the screams and trampling sounds from the boatful of hapless humanity. The conflagration brightened the night as if it were day.

A stiff breeze blew searing heat and smoke into her face, causing Rosaleen to cough. Earlier, she'd decided she would die before she allowed Bill and his gambling cronies to have their way with her another night. Now, death seemed a distinct possibility. She glanced at the spreading flames behind her then down at the dark cold waters of the Ohio River beneath her. Grasping the riverboat's rail, she wondered which would be the easier way to die.

"Rosaleen! Rosaleen!"

The sound of Bill's voice barking from somewhere in the darkness sealed her decision. Gulping a lungful of smoke-laced air, she vaulted over the rail.

Hitting the cold water, she gasped, the enveloping river causing her to lose precious oxygen. The wet heaviness of her clothes pulled her down farther into the dark depths of the Ohio River.

Black. Pitch-black.

Her burning lungs felt as if they might explode. How easy

to just open her mouth and surrender to the death she'd contemplated only an hour earlier. Yet as fear wrapped her heart in its crippling grasp, panic sprang from deep within her, bursting into a determined resolve. She wanted to live.

The terror in her heart turned to anger. She wouldn't let the river take her. Given this chance of escape, she'd not surrender to death without a fight.

Her arms flailing, she kicked out her legs bound by the heavy wet folds of her skirt and petticoats. Her head emerged from the water, and she sucked in grateful gulps of air. Blinking water from her eyes, she continued to kick her legs while pushing and pulling her arms, treading water just as Papa had taught her years ago.

She looked through the darkness at the blazing riverboat, now several yards away. The orange flames licked at the night sky. Unearthly screams filled the air. Curses blended with prayers, causing her to wonder if she really had died and this was hell.

She could hear splashes that indicated other passengers were also abandoning certain death on the *Cortland Belle*, choosing to seek dubious refuge in the river. Was Bill McGurty among them?

Rosaleen's shivers had little to do with the cold water. She pushed her arms harder, attempting to put more distance between herself and the boat. Her legs fought the strong current as the undertow threatened to pull her beneath the surface.

As frightening and uncertain as the dark abyss of death seemed, Black Jack Bill McGurty was far more terrifying.

Donovan had been a good man. If heaven existed, surely Donovan had gone there. Maybe if she begged God—if there *was* a God—He'd take her to Donovan. Even if she was undeserving, they'd been married. Didn't that mean they belonged together?

A sob tore from her smoke-filled throat. *Oh God, if You're really out there somewhere and can hear me, if I die, please take me to Donovan.*

∾

Oh Lord, I can only wonder how many died without knowing You.

The prayer rose from Jacob Hale's heavy heart. Standing at the corner of Broadway and Second Street, he gazed through the early morning mist toward the Ohio River. There, in the dark of the previous night, unnumbered souls had glimpsed this world for the last time, propelled into the next by the explosion of the steamboat's boiler and subsequent blaze.

Sighing, he set his toolbox in the shade of the old willow. Its supple green tresses of new spring foliage were bent as if in sorrowful benediction.

It bothered him to think that bodies still lay beneath the river with nothing to mark their watery graves. Hopefully, all could be recovered, identified, and given Christian burials. But sadly he knew that often, after such accidents, bodies remained trapped under debris or were swept downriver by the current.

He looked down at the modest, flat stone caressed by the willow's tender branches. "At least, my old friend, you have a marker."

REV. ORVILLE WHITAKER, B.1782 D.1845.

Two months ago, Jacob had buried his friend and mentor on the plot they'd planned for the new church. His gaze swept over the nearly completed foundation. "It should be finished by the end of the summer, Orville."

Jacob liked to imagine his friend looking down from heaven and smiling upon his efforts.

The congregation Orville had established still met on Sunday mornings in Opal Buchanan's boardinghouse parlor to hear Jacob's sermons. But God willing, they'd be listening to them this fall from pews in this church he was helping to build with his own hands.

Jacob's gaze drifted back to the river, his thoughts turning once more to the steamboat accident. The sound of the explosion had jolted him awake. Although he'd hurried to join others from the Fair Play Fire Company, he'd soon returned home, realizing nothing could be done to save the doomed steamboat.

Compelled to be nearer the scene of last night's tragedy, he walked a block down Broadway to Ohio Street and the river's edge. A lingering smell of wood smoke clung to the morning air, competing with the odors of Madison, Indiana's pork-packing industry.

He looked across the river's surface glinting in the morning sun to the charred remains of what had been the steamboat *Cortland Belle*. Listing hard starboard, it lay snagged on a sandbar near the Kentucky shore. Blackened, jagged pieces of the boat, along with unidentifiable debris, littered the water.

Jacob said a prayer for the souls of those who'd died in the accident then blew out a long, deep sigh. *Many others are still alive and could hear the Word before it's too late—*

His musings were cut short when he caught sight of an odd-looking object a few yards to his left down a sandy embankment. Curious, he made his way toward what looked like a purple bundle. As he drew nearer, his heart sank.

The body of a woman lay half hidden amid a cluster of sapling willows. He could see she was only partially out of the river with her legs still in the water, swathed in the wet folds of her purple dress. She lay facedown, her hair splayed out around her head, covering her features. The sun shone on the wavy, mahogany-colored strands, revealing tinges of burnished copper.

What beautiful hair.

The thought pricked Jacob's conscience the moment it formed in his mind. This had been a person. Someone's daughter. Perhaps someone's wife. Most probably, a victim of the riverboat explosion. She would need a Christian burial. He reached a tentative hand out toward her shoulder.

Oh Lord, I don't want to do this.

He'd seen several dead bodies in his twenty-six years of life, but it never got any easier. Jacob grasped her shoulder to turn her over.

She groaned, causing him to jump back in surprise.

As the morning sun touched her features, he detected a faint blush of pink staining her pale cheeks and full lips. This was no dead body!

Heart pounding, he dropped to his knees beside the woman. Taking her cool hands into his, he began rubbing warmth into her long, delicate fingers.

Her eyelids, fringed by thick dark lashes, fluttered open.

Slipping his left arm beneath her back, Jacob lifted her head and upper torso from the riverbank. "It's all right. You're going to be all right," he assured her, brushing hair and sand from her face with his free hand.

Her lips parted to emit another soft groan.

Jacob wrenched his attention from the arresting beauty of the woman to focus upon her plight. "You'll be all right now," he repeated. "I'm going to take care of you."

She blinked several times before squinting blue-green eyes against the morning sun. "Donovan? Is that you, Donovan?" It was all she managed to mumble before her eyes closed again.

Lowering her to the riverbank, he anxiously pressed his fingers against her throat just below her jaw. A strong pulse beneath his touch brought him a measure of relief.

Ephraim. I need to get her to Ephraim.

Hurrying back up Broadway, he fetched his mule-drawn wagon full of lumber down to Ohio Street then carried the woman up to his wagon.

Dear Lord, please just let her live.

As gently as possible, Jacob laid her on the two-by-sixes in the wagon bed. He climbed to the wagon seat and slapped the reins down hard onto the mules' backs. "Heyaa!" he yelled, urging the animals to a quickened pace up Broadway toward Main-Cross Street.

two

A strong smell of camphor caused Rosaleen to jerk awake. She blinked and the image of a man came into focus.

"Ah, there you are." The tall, dark-haired man smiled as he waved the offensive-smelling bottle in front of her nose.

Where was she? How had she gotten here? Confused, she cast quick glances around the room. A large green cabinet sat against one wall. Corked bottles holding varying colors of liquids and powders crowded on four shelves behind the cabinet's glass doors.

The man picked up a trumpet-shaped object from a sideboard. "I am Dr. Morgan and, with your permission, I'd like to check the strength of your heartbeat."

Rosaleen nodded her assent, and he pressed the broader end of the instrument against her chest while holding the small, ivory-colored end to his ear.

"Well," he said, laying aside the instrument, "other than some bruising and exhaustion, I can find no injuries."

"Wh–where am I?" Disoriented, Rosaleen attempted to rise from a large, leather-upholstered chair.

A woman she hadn't noticed before gently restrained her. Dark brown curls peeked from beneath the white cotton cap framing the woman's pleasant face. "You're all right, dear. You're in Madison, Indiana, in Dr. Ephraim Morgan's office. I'm his wife, Becky Morgan." The kindness in the woman's soothing voice helped to quell Rosaleen's anxiety.

Sinking back into the chair, she submitted to the pressure of Mrs. Morgan's gentle grasp on her shoulders.

"You've been through an awful ordeal, but you are safe now." The woman's bright blue eyes conveyed assurance above an encouraging smile as she smoothed the white starched apron covering her blue calico day dress.

Still trying to make sense of it all, Rosaleen paid scant attention when the doctor's wife walked to a side door. Opening it, Mrs. Morgan spoke quiet, unintelligible words in a summoning tone.

"How did. . . How did I get. . . ?" Rosaleen murmured. Suddenly, it all flooded back into her consciousness with dizzying speed. The explosion. The fire. Bill.

She remembered the sun's warmth on her face and a man with light hair. Donovan? No. Donovan was dead. Had she been visited by an angel? *Do angels really exist?*

"I found you on the riverbank. Thought you. . .hadn't made it." The voice that answered her fractured question belonged to the figure of a second man who'd just entered the room.

Following the sound of his voice, Rosaleen blinked again as the man moved from the glare of the window.

Dressed as a common laborer, he wore a pair of black wool work trousers and a white work shirt. The shirt's sleeves, rolled above his elbows, revealed tanned, muscular arms. His vivid blue eyes, so like those of the woman who'd comforted her, peered intently into her face. It was his hair, however, that helped untangle her snarled memories. A shock of thick, light hair framed his tanned features.

Her "angel."

"Do you have any family we should contact?" The man took a step nearer.

For a moment she sat mute, gazing at her rescuer. "Family?" The stern features of Wilfred and Irene Maguire swam before her eyes. "No." She heard the word leave her lips on a sad whisper. "I have no family who cares for me."

"No husband?" The blond young man shot a quizzical glance at her gold wedding ring on her left hand.

"Dead." Tears sprang to Rosaleen's eyes at the awful memory of Donovan slumping over the card table, his blood spreading a maroon stain across its green felt top.

"Others survived the explosion," the doctor interjected

with an encouraging lilt. "Most survivors were rescued on the Kentucky side of the river, but I treated a few last night. What was your husband's name?" He turned to his wife. "Becky, love, would you please get the record book?"

Mrs. Morgan stepped toward a large mahogany desk at the end of the room.

"No." Rosaleen's definitive tone arrested the woman's slight, energetic form. "He's dead. I watched him die." Caving beneath the weight of all that had happened to her in the past months, Rosaleen pressed her hands to her face and wept.

"Oh, you poor dear." The doctor's wife rushed to Rosaleen's side, gathering her in a lye-soap-and-verbena-scented embrace.

Allowing her body to sway with the woman's rocking, Rosaleen sobbed, eagerly embracing the genuine caring she'd craved since Donovan's death.

When her tears subsided, Rosaleen twisted in Mrs. Morgan's arms, sniffed, and gazed up at her "angel."

"I'm so sorry for your loss, ma'am. Jacob Hale, at your service." He dipped a quick bow. "I'm Mrs. Morgan's brother," he added. "And you are. . ."

"Rosaleen. Rosaleen Archer."

"Well, you'll need somewhere to stay." Mrs. Morgan's tone solidified. "You must stay with us."

Dr. Morgan turned to his wife with a rueful shake of his head. "Darling, you know I would normally encourage such a philanthropic notion, but think, there is nowhere at the moment we could comfortably situate a house guest."

His wife's sigh conveyed her regret. "Of course you're right, my dear. With the upstairs being renovated, we do well to manage accommodations for ourselves and the children."

"I wouldn't want to intrude. I'm sure there must be somewhere. . ." Without the prospect of a roof over her head, Rosaleen battled a resurgence of panic.

"Mrs. Buchanan has a spare attic room at the boardinghouse at the moment. She's also been looking for an extra hired girl now that Patsey is in the family way." The corner of Jacob

Hale's mouth quirked in an encouraging smile. "I'm sure I could work something out."

At his steady gaze, Rosaleen's heart quickened. She scolded herself sternly. *I can't make attachments. I must get away from here as soon as I can. I must get away from the river.*

⋆

Riding on the wagon seat beside Jacob Hale, Rosaleen took in the town of Madison. Cradled between the Ohio River to the south and steep, stony hills to the east and north, the "Porkopolis" seemed focused on the river to which it owed its prosperity.

She'd passed the place many times on riverboats yet had never disembarked here. Once, Donovan had pointed out the town to her from the pilothouse of a sternwheeler. He'd explained that most of the pork in the country was packed at Madison, Indiana.

As they traveled down a street marked Main-Cross, the smooth gravel paving the extraordinarily wide thoroughfare crunched beneath the wagon's iron-rimmed wheels. A couple of blocks beyond the doctor's house, the neat two-story brick houses lining the street gave way to bustling shops—all brick.

"Is everything made of brick here?" she asked, voicing her thoughts.

"Almost." His lips curved in a grin. "Five years ago the town adopted an ordinance requiring all new buildings be bricked in order to cut down on fires."

As they turned left onto a much narrower street, panic clenched her insides as tightly as her laced fingers whitening in her lap. What if the Buchanan woman didn't accept her? *What if—*

"Opal Buchanan is a good woman," Jacob Hale said with a kind smile as if he'd read her thoughts. "Her husband, a coffee merchant, died of dropsy six years ago. After George's death, she sold the business and opened her home as a boardinghouse. Well, here we are." He pulled the mules to a halt in front of a two-story home.

The brick facade of the boardinghouse looked unpretentious in its coat of gray paint. It seemed warm and homey. Its white-pillared porch reached out a welcoming greeting.

Rosaleen felt safe—a feeling that had been absent in her life during the six months since Donovan's murder.

A small brass bell at the top of the front door jingled as Jacob Hale ushered her into a front hall brightened by the opaque glass of a transom window.

The warm, comforting aroma of freshly baked bread greeted them, causing Rosaleen's stomach to grind with hunger. She soon heard the sound of quick footsteps, and a tall, large-boned woman appeared, smoothing back her graying blond hair.

Jacob Hale glanced from the woman to Rosaleen. "Mrs. Buchanan, may I introduce Mrs. Rosaleen Archer. She's a survivor from last night's riverboat explosion."

Feeling Jacob Hale's reassuring hand against her back, Rosaleen watched the woman's curious smile fade to a look of sympathy.

Mrs. Buchanan's kind green gaze seemed to flit over Rosaleen. "You poor soul, please come in and sit." The woman reached out her substantial arm and encircled Rosaleen's waist, quickly whisking her into a sunny parlor.

Stunned by Mrs. Buchanan's swift action, Rosaleen glanced back at her rescuer, left standing in the front hall.

Jacob Hale met her look with an amused grin.

Entering the parlor, Rosaleen took in the room. Larger than she would have expected for this size of house, the parlor testified to the success of the late Mr. Buchanan's business. Rich India carpets of green and gold hues dotted the floor. The room showcased several pieces of nice furniture, including a horsehair sofa, carved mahogany tables, as well as silk- and velvet-upholstered chairs and settees.

"You must be starving, poor thing. I'll bring you a nice big glass of milk and some thick buttered slices of Patsey's fresh bread." The woman seemed adept at taking charge and obviously relished the position. "You sit right down here." Mrs. Buchanan guided her toward a green velvet settee, pooh-poohing Rosaleen's concerns about her skirt soiled with river mud.

"Mrs. Archer lost her husband in the accident and has no other family or place to stay," Jacob said as he entered the parlor. "You'd mentioned you were looking for another hired girl. Mrs. Archer is willing to take the job in exchange for the use of the attic room."

Rosaleen didn't correct the man. Perhaps it would be better for them to think that Donovan had died in the explosion.

Opal Buchanan gave a sympathetic gasp and pressed her hand to her heart. "A widow, and so young. Why, you can scarcely be out of your teens."

"Twenty," Rosaleen supplied.

Opal glanced up at Jacob. "Yes, of course she can have the attic, but that little room is hardly more than a closet with only a straw mattress on the floor." She turned back to Rosaleen. "I wish I could do better for you, dear, and you shall be paid besides. That is, as soon as you feel up to any work." The woman clasped Rosaleen's hands in her large ones, giving them a quick, warm squeeze.

Rosaleen's helpless gaze traveled from one to the other as she wiped grateful tears from her cheeks with the lace handkerchief Mrs. Buchanan pressed into her hand. "I don't know how to thank you both. I—"

"Now, now, dear." Opal Buchanan patted her shoulder. "We are doing no more than what our Lord has asked of us. Isn't that right, Reverend Hale?"

A preacher?

Dread knotted Rosaleen's insides, and her heart raced. She let the kerchief drop to her lap. Her eyes widening, she raised her face to Jacob Hale's.

"That's right, Opal." He smiled and dipped a bow. "Mrs. Archer, I shall leave you in Opal's capable hands and see you at supper." When his eyes—the color of an October sky—

gazed deeply into hers, Rosaleen caught her breath.

"And don't you be late, Reverend." Rosaleen heard a measure of affection in Opal Buchanan's teasing tone. "A preacher, and he's the only one of my boarders who's ever late for supper." With a soft chuckle, Opal left the room shaking her head.

While she waited on the settee for Mrs. Buchanan's promised bread and milk, a thread of disappointment embroidered the trepidation wrapping around Rosaleen's heart. Reverend Wilfred Maguire's disapproving countenance floated before her eyes. Her gaze dropped to the rose-patterned rug in the parlor doorway vacated only moments before by her handsome rescuer.

A preacher! Why did he have to be a preacher?

three

"Reckon this oughta 'bout do it, Rev'rend." Freedman Andrew Chapman stood near the parlor door and mopped at his dark, sweaty forehead with a tattered kerchief.

Jacob straightened after helping Andrew place the last of a dozen two-by-eights across rows of low trestles. His slow gaze swept Mrs. Buchanan's rearranged parlor. The sofa and settee made up the first row, followed by an odd collection of five chairs. Behind the chairs came the rows of plank seating. "Actually, Andrew, my fervent prayer is that it *won't* be enough." Jacob met the tall young black man's wide grin with one of his own.

In the year since he and Orville Whitaker had begun holding services in Opal Buchanan's boardinghouse, their congregation had doubled from an average of ten to twenty. "I've planned the sanctuary of the new church to accommodate over one hundred. Orville always told me to never limit God. 'Think big, build big, and He will fill it big.'"

Andrew nodded. "Amen to that, Rev'rend. The Lord'll provide the crop. It's up to us to do the harvestin'."

The resurgence of a nagging concern caused Jacob's smile to sag with his heart. The relentless doubt that constantly gnawed at his confidence whispered its insidious charge. *You've not had one convert since Orville's death. Perhaps this is not your calling. Perhaps God has not anointed you.*

Adding to his uncertainty, the one person he'd worked the hardest to bring into the fold continued to resist his efforts. Rosaleen Archer always seemed to find something else she needed to do on Sunday mornings rather than attend his services.

Andrew's chest puffed out with pride. "Well, reckon me and

Patsey are doin' our part to add another soul to our church up at Georgetown. The babe oughta be comin' along in the fall, 'bout the time we get your church built."

"Be fruitful and multiply, Andrew." Jacob chuckled, giving his friend a slap on the back.

How wonderful it would be to have a helpmate. Before, thoughts of marriage had conjured little more than a vague idea in Jacob's mind—a faceless lady offering support, love, and an equal commitment to winning souls for the Lord as she worked tirelessly by his side. Three weeks ago, that image had been given a face.

The fact that Rosaleen showed no sign of interest in the Lord, or His work, caused a painful tug-of-war inside Jacob. He understood her pain and respected her loss. But living in the same boardinghouse, exposed to her beauty and industry day after day, he could not deny his attraction to the lovely young widow.

The words of 2 Corinthians 6:14 tortured Jacob's mind and heart: *Be ye not unequally yoked together with unbelievers.*

If only she'd come once and hear the Word. *If only. . .*

"Patsey says she needs more wood for the kitchen stove, Andrew."

Jacob's head jerked with his heart. Heat spread from his neck to his face. The subject of his thoughts stood in the parlor doorway. Rich brown tendrils had escaped her snowy daycap and curled appealingly against her rosy cheeks.

Laughing, Andrew shook his head and walked toward the kitchen. "That woman ain't content 'less I'm either choppin' or fetchin' wood."

Rosaleen turned to follow Andrew.

"Rosaleen. . ." His heart thumping, Jacob managed her name, stopping her at the threshold between the door and hallway.

She turned back to face him with a questioning look.

"I'm hoping that maybe you could put aside time tomorrow morning to attend services. I've prepared a sermon dealing with God's peace and love in times of grief. I thought if you're ready, it might help. . . ." Fearing he was completely botching the invitation, Jacob's heart lifted when she rewarded his attempt with a sad, sweet smile.

"Reverend Hale, I'm sure it is a very fine sermon." The touch of her hand on his forearm sent shivers racing to Jacob's shoulder. "I just don't see any sense to it. I mean, I don't see what good the scriptures could do *me*."

"Oh, Rosaleen, just open your heart. God wants to comfort you. All of us here want to comfort you, too."

The tears welling in her beautiful blue-green eyes ripped at his heart. *Please, Lord, give me the words.* "Won't you just come and listen?"

"I don't know," she answered just above a whisper.

He watched her lovely lips tremble as a tear slipped down her cheek. It took all his strength to not pull her into his arms. Instead, he clasped her hands in his. "I hope you will consider it." He forced a smile. "I'd love to see you in the congregation."

Disappointment twanged inside him when she pulled her hands from his, turned, and left the parlor.

⁊⁊

In the darkness of her tiny attic room, Rosaleen sat bolt upright on her straw mattress. A cold sweat beaded on her forehead, and her breath came in painful puffs. Someone had screamed. She hugged the voluminous nightdress against her shaking body and realized her own throat had made the awful sound.

"Rosaleen? Rosaleen, are you all right?" Jacob Hale's frantic plea came from just outside her door.

"I–I'm fine." She fought to keep her voice steady. "Just a night terror."

"Would you like to talk?"

"No, thank you. I'm fine. I'm fine."

Fine in no way described how Rosaleen felt. Yet she couldn't bring herself to share with Jacob Hale the horrors that had caused her screams. He considered her a respectable widow.

She loathed the thought of shattering that image. However, just hearing his voice and knowing he stood outside her door helped to chase away the terror lurking in the dark corners of her mind.

"If you're sure you're all right. . ." The hesitancy in his voice caused a sweet ache deep inside her.

She heard a flurry of footfalls on the steps leading to her attic room, followed by Opal Buchanan's concerned voice. "What's wrong?"

"Just a nightmare, Mrs. Buchanan. Everything is fine." Rosaleen could hear Jacob's quiet voice reassuring Opal, interrupted by Tobias Stilwell's surly tone.

"Can't get a decent night's sleep around this place. Thought somebody'd been murdered." The salesman's deep-throated grumble faded down the creaking stairway.

"Rosaleen, dear. If there's anything you need. . ."

"No, thank you, Opal. I'm fine. I'm sorry I bothered everyone's sleep."

"Nonsense, dear. You've been through an awful experience. The steamboat. . .your husband. . ." Opal's voice faltered with her attempt at consolation.

Quiet, unintelligible whispers preceded the sound of Opal's slow, heavy footsteps on the stairs.

"Any time you need to talk, I'm here."

"Thank you, Reverend. I'm sorry I—"

"Any time, Rosaleen." She heard a smile creep into his voice. "Please call me Jacob. I much prefer it."

"Thank you. . .Jacob."

Long after the sound of his footsteps had faded away, she shifted on her mattress, sleep eluding her. She'd tried to ignore her attraction to the handsome young minister, but with each passing day, his grasp on her heart grew tighter.

Didn't he know she was irretrievably beyond the realm of salvation? Reverend Wilfred Maguire had called her "irredeemable—the wicked by-blow of a harlot." Surely, he— the minister of a huge church in Natchez, Mississippi—knew the scriptures better than a poor, young backwoods preacher.

If God rejects me, then I shall reject God!

Rosaleen squeezed her eyes shut tight against the tears oozing through her lashes. For all she knew, nothing but oblivion awaited her beyond this life. So she must make the best of it—find what happiness she could while she lived.

She patted the place in the mattress where she'd made a small slit and pushed in the calico pouch holding her three-week earnings. The reassuring *clink* of coins rubbing against one another lent a measure of hope to her heart.

When she'd earned enough money, she must make her way to Maestro Levitsky in New York and her dream of becoming a concert pianist.

Besides, she had no way of knowing for sure if Bill McGurty had survived the accident or gone down with the steamboat. Perhaps he was looking for her on the Kentucky side of the river—or he could be in Madison this very minute. A shudder wriggled through her.

Anyway, the last place he'd expect to find me would be in the company of churchgoing people.

Calmed by the thought, she reached into the slit in the mattress. Feeling through the prickly straw, she wrapped her fingers around the sack that held her hope.

four

"That man o' mine sure outdid hisself with this mess of squirrels." Patsey beamed at the two large crocks filled with butchered squirrel parts covered in brine.

From the first day Jacob brought her to Opal Buchanan's boardinghouse, Rosaleen had found a true friend in Patsey Chapman. In fact, Mrs. Buchanan's pretty hired girl with skin the color of rich cocoa had welcomed her with open arms. About her own age, with an unquenchable, bubbly personality, Patsey had helped Rosaleen reclaim the joy of being young.

"I've never eaten squirrel." Rosaleen lobbed a spoonful of lard into the hot cast-iron skillet on the stove, unsure of how she felt about the supper entrée.

"Then you're in for a real treat. I growed up on squirrel down where I come from. It's gener'ly my favorite. But right now"—she laughed as she patted the mound beneath her calico apron—"I cain't even abide the smell of meat."

"You're not from here?"

"No." A dusty white cloud rose as Patsey dumped a handful of squirrel into another crockery bowl filled with flour and seasoning. Her bright, dark eyes grew round, and her voice dropped to a conspiratorial whisper. "My mammy an' me 'scaped from Williamsburg, Kentucky, and come up here on the Railroad a couple years ago."

Rosaleen realized she wasn't talking about any sort of conveyance that moved on rails. She'd heard whispers of the Underground Railroad in the month she'd been in Madison and suspected the town was a stop on escaped slaves' routes north to Canada. She'd learned that the Georgetown district where Patsey and Andrew lived, just two blocks east of the boardinghouse, was the free black section of town. There, men like the barber, George de Baptiste, and the blacksmith, Elijah Anderson, were leaders in the work of the Underground. She also suspected that Mrs. Buchanan actively helped in the humanitarian effort.

"When we got here to the Georgetown district, Andrew was one of 'em helpin' to find us places to stay and food to eat." Her teeth flashed like pearls amid the grin stretching her rosy brown cheeks. "He was the finest-lookin' man I ever did see."

Rosaleen grinned. "Then it was love at first sight?"

"Was for me." Patsey smiled. "And I reckon I'd have pined the rest of my life for him if I hadn't took sick with a fever, keepin' me and Mammy from movin' on to the next station. We stayed a month with Andrew and his folks till my fever passed."

"And you and Andrew fell in love?"

Patsey nodded, her smile quirking into a grin. "Andrew wouldn't admit it, but I think he was feared o' lovin' me, knowin' I'd be movin' on."

"But you didn't."

"No." Her brow creased, and Rosaleen could see she was remembering the emotional struggle. "Mammy begged me to go on with her up north to Indianapolis. Said this was way too close to the line."

Rosaleen knew that along this stretch of the Ohio, the river itself was the line between slave and free country. Many whites here were more than willing to turn blacks over to their slaveholders for the bounty.

"But when Andrew got up the nerve and asked me to stay and jump the broom with him, I couldn't say no." Patsey's face lit and her eyes sparkled with love. "Never been sorry. He's as purty inside as out," she said grinning. Handing Rosaleen the crock of floured squirrel, she shot her a curious glance. "Did you love your man?"

Unprepared for the question, Rosaleen allowed a long moment of silence while she busied herself positioning the sizzling meat in the skillet with extra care. "No." She felt a pang of guilt at the whispered word.

The question had been one she'd shied away from for a long time. She glanced at Patsey's face, still glowing at the mere mention of Andrew.

Rosaleen thought of the man thirteen years her senior to whom she'd been wed for six short weeks. Although he had been a kind and gentle husband, thoughts of Donovan Archer had never quickened her heart. Since her father's death, the short time she'd spent with Donovan had been the one brief splash of contentment in her life. But in her heart she knew she'd never felt true love for him.

"You're young. You got plenty of time." The kind, almost pitying tone of Patsey's voice caused Rosaleen to blink away tears.

Nodding, Rosaleen felt a stab of envy.

Patsey's voice took on a teasing lilt. "I done seen the way Rev'rend Hale looks at you. His eyes goin' all moon-calf-like. Done seen the way you look at him, too." She danced around the little kitchen in an exaggerated sashay, holding out the sides of her calico skirt with dusty hands. "Jis a few winks and nods, and you'd have him askin' you to jump the broom."

"Patsey Chapman!" Heat that had nothing to do with the frying pan rushed to Rosaleen's face. Had she been so transparent about her feelings for Jacob? Could Patsey be right about Jacob? It didn't matter. Unlike Patsey, she couldn't stay. "I have no designs on Reverend Hale, and I'm sure he has no interest in me that way either."

Patsey gave an indelicate snort and laughed. "Well, you have it your way, but I jis know what I done seen, that's all." Then, with a low moan, she waved her hand at the gamy meat and sage-laced steam rising from the skillet. Holding her stomach with one hand, she pressed the other against her mouth. "Lord, help me! I cain't abide another minute of that smell," she mumbled through her hand. "I best peel these taters outside." Snatching a wooden bowl full of potatoes from the table, she retreated toward the kitchen door.

Gazing through the open door, Rosaleen watched the young woman settle herself on a stool beneath an oak tree to pare the potatoes. She told herself that Patsey's notion sprang simply from her romantic imagination, yet there was a part of her that hoped it hadn't.

&

"Mmm, squirrel." Jacob inhaled deeply when Rosaleen brought the platter heaped with the golden brown pieces of meat to the supper table. "I've been looking forward to this since Andrew told me what luck he'd had hunting."

Rosaleen's heart quickened beneath Jacob's lingering gaze.

"Smells like you've done a wonderful job with them," Jacob commented to her.

"And how do you know Patsey didn't cook these?" His bright blue eyes fixed on hers drained the strength from her arms, and she hurried to set down the platter.

"Because Andrew told me he was afraid he might not get any as the smell of meat makes Patsey ill now."

"Then I suppose I'm the one to blame if they are not cooked well," Rosaleen said with a grin. She was finding it increasingly difficult to disavow Patsey's claim.

"Squirrel! I haven't had squirrel since—Well, I can't remember when I last had squirrel." Rosaleen gave an inward groan when Tobias Stilwell dropped his lanky frame onto a dining room chair.

A look of dismay replaced the smile on Jacob's face.

Since his appearance two weeks ago, the cookstove salesman had not ingratiated himself to anyone at the boardinghouse. His habits rivaled the worst Rosaleen had seen during her years aboard the steamboats. Except at mealtime, he perpetually kept a wad of chewing tobacco in his jaw. He'd continually spit the foul-smelling brown juice in the general direction of the nearest spittoon, seemingly unconcerned whether he hit the mark. Worse, the looks he raked over Rosaleen gave her cold chills and caused her to lock her attic room door at night.

Good-hearted Opal Buchanan couldn't seem to bring herself to send the unsavory character on his way, even though his promised payment for room and board had yet to materialize.

"Rosaleen, do you remember how many squirrels you fried up?" Jacob's tone sounded benign, but Rosaleen caught a mischievous glint in his eyes.

She'd learned in the past month that Jacob Hale had a penchant for practical jokes. She remembered how Opal had laughed, recounting that she'd once made the mistake of teasing him about always being the preacher and never taking a day off. Later that day, she'd discovered all her candles missing from their holders. After searching the house over, she'd found them under a bushel basket turned upside down on the back porch. Opal told her Jacob later confessed to the prank, saying he was attempting to make a point about a verse in the Gospel of Matthew. Rosaleen couldn't remember the scripture Opal quoted, but it had something to do with not hiding a light under a bushel basket but putting it on a candlestick so it would light the house.

"No, I never actually counted the squirrels," Rosaleen answered Jacob, unsure of his intention but keen to play along.

"Andrew said he killed six squirrels, but that sure looks like more. Hmmm," he said thoughtfully. "By the way, have you seen that tortoiseshell cat that's been bedeviling Mrs. Buchanan? I heard her tell Andrew she wanted him to get rid of that thing one way or another."

"Now that you mention it, I haven't seen it at all today." Rosaleen fought to keep a straight face, realizing what Jacob was up to. She'd learned that the one thing Opal Buchanan and Tobias Stilwell had in common was their mutual disdain for the feline species.

"One, two, three—" His face wearing a deadly serious expression, Jacob poked a fork at the golden brown pieces of fried squirrel.

Tobias had become very still. Rosaleen ventured a glance in

his direction and was forced to press a napkin to her mouth. The salesman's eyes began growing large, and his pinched features took on a greenish pallor all the way up to his balding pate.

"Andrew must have counted wrong, because I'm counting legs and back pieces for seven animals," Jacob concluded.

Tobias Stilwell practically leaped from his chair, causing it to fall backward with a thud. "I—I'm not really hungry. I—I just remembered I have an appointment in Cincinnati day after tomorrow." His hand shook as he righted the chair and mumbled, "Please give Mrs. Buchanan my regrets and tell her I'll be sending my payment."

"What's gotten into him?" Opal Buchanan carried a plateful of cornbread into the dining room just in time to see Tobias race out.

"Suddenly remembered an important engagement," Jacob told her with a poker face as good as any Rosaleen had ever witnessed. He gave a deep, soulful sigh. "Alas, I'm afraid we will no longer be enjoying Mr. Stilwell's stellar company."

"Thank the Lord! I've been praying for this for two solid weeks." Opal sank to a chair, relief blooming on her face.

"Prayer works, Opal. All it takes is a little faith." Jacob's eyes lit as a sudden thought seemed to ignite behind them. He turned an impish grin toward Rosaleen. "I just decided on my theme for Sunday's sermon. 'Faith without works is dead.'"

Rosaleen allowed her gaze to meet Jacob's, dancing with fun. As they shared a secret grin, she acknowledged the truth screaming from her heart.

How am I going to leave now that I know Patsey is right?

five

"Rosaleen."

Jacob's quiet voice caused Rosaleen's heart to thump. She turned toward the parlor doorway, her feather duster poised in midair.

She'd been careful not to enter the parlor until she felt sure he'd gone to the church building site. If she were to squelch her blossoming feelings for the preacher, Rosaleen knew she must avoid him whenever possible.

"I was wondering if you might like to accompany me to my sister's home for a visit this afternoon."

A small burst of panic flared inside her. How could she trust her heart to behave during an entire afternoon in Jacob's company? "I—I have chores to do. Opal expects—"

"Opal's already told me it would be fine." His blue eyes twinkled into hers. "She says you've been cooped up in this house for the last month and need to get out more. I agree."

Rosaleen had to admit it would be nice to get away from the boardinghouse for a while. Her self-imposed confinement here had ceased to feel as much like protection as incarceration. But she needed to stay detached from Madison—from Jacob. She must find some excuse. Any excuse.

She glanced down at the patched calico dress Patsey had loaned her. "I have nothing decent to wear for a social call."

"And that is precisely the reason you need to visit Becky. She told me she's found a few of her dresses from last summer that are a little too snug since the birth of my niece, Lucy. She's sure they will fit you perfectly."

Rosaleen stiffened. She didn't like being considered a charity case. Worse, she did not want to feel beholden to Jacob's sister. "From what I remember, your sister looked very trim. I'd think with a small alteration. . ."

Jacob's grin suggested he had no plans to cede the argument. "My guess is Becky's glad for an excuse to buy new dresses." His smile softened with his tone. He took her hand in his. Rosaleen's heart began racing at his touch.

"Rosaleen, Becky wants to help you. We all want to help you. We believe that helping others is the same as helping our Lord. Jesus tells us in Matthew 25:40, 'Inasmuch as ye have done it unto one of the least of these my brethren, ye have done it unto me.'"

The kind look in his eyes eroded her resolve.

"Please, Rosaleen, allow Becky to help you. Allow us all to help you."

Rosaleen swallowed hard and blinked back tears. Kindness, charity, and generosity were qualities she'd rarely encountered. She returned to dusting the cherry table that no longer needed it. "I still have nothing fit to wear."

"Mrs. Buchanan was able to salvage that purple frock you were wearing when I found you." His gaze held hers in a tender embrace and her heart stood still. "Whatever you wear, you will look fetching."

A half hour later, Rosaleen stood in Opal Buchanan's bedchamber, the yards of purple silk rustling as she shook out the dress. Though water stained and with a bodice cut far too low to be proper for day wear, it was the best she had.

After donning the dress, Rosaleen stood before the dresser mirror, her heart aflutter. Opal had managed to brush away all visible remnants of river mud. Rosaleen had to admit, aside from its inappropriate style and damaged condition, the dress did flatter her coloring.

Three times she twisted her auburn locks into a figure-eight bun without complete satisfaction. Grimacing her dismay, she covered her unruly hair with the gray silk bonnet Opal had loaned her.

It's only Jacob. I see him every day.

The silent admonitions did little to calm Rosaleen's

palpitating heart. What she saw in the cherrywood-framed mirror only added to her unease. The image of a saloon girl mocked her from the glass.

Soiled dove.

Rosaleen's face burned with grief and shame. *Not because I wanted it. Never, never. . .*

She choked back a sob and felt the tentative grasp she'd had on her nerve slip.

During her time with Bill McGurty, the looks she'd gotten from respectable people had stung. Their furtive glances had seemed a mixture of disgust and morbid curiosity. Aboard the steamboats, mothers had nervously shooed their children past her while gentlemen openly ogled her when their wives were not looking.

It had brought back all the cruel taunts and snide comments she'd endured from upper-class girls at Mrs. Griswold's Academy after they learned of her illegitimacy. Those hurtful jeers blended with Wilfred and Irene Maguire's disparaging description of her as "the filthy little spawn of a harlot."

Rosaleen drew a deep breath and, with trembling hands, wrapped Opal's black lace shawl around her shoulders left bare by the dress's revealing bodice. Her heart pounding, she headed down the stairs.

"You look lovely." At the bottom step, Jacob greeted her with a deep bow, a bell-crowned white beaver hat in his hand. He looked every inch a gentleman in his maroon claw-hammer coat over a buff waistcoat, satin neckerchief, and close-fitting black trousers. Yet the eager anticipation sparkling in his blue eyes lent an irresistible boyish charm to his features. Even the thin scar running parallel to his left cheekbone added to, rather than detracted from, his good looks.

As they strolled along the boardwalk edging Main-Cross Street, Rosaleen's gaze took in the beauty of the little river town. Graceful oaks, sycamores, and maples lined the street, shading its broad expanse of smooth gravel.

"Ah, here we are." Jacob's smile widened when they neared a two-story brick home.

A fragrant greeting wafted their way from phlox, larkspurs, and petunias growing beneath the two tall, narrow windows. Left of the windows, two white-painted pillars supported a corniced portico jutting out from a recessed doorway.

"You're sure we are not intruding upon your sister's time?" Rosaleen's stomach felt the flutter of nervous butterflies as the wrought iron gate creaked a tiny protest against Jacob's hand.

"Nonsense. Becky has been pestering me about you for the past month. And since you refuse to attend Sunday services," he teased with a quirk of his mouth, "I decided an afternoon visit was in order."

Rosaleen's heart quickened at the reassuring touch of his hand on her back, guiding her up the two stone steps to the little enclosed portico.

"Mrs. Archer." A bright smile lit Becky Morgan's face when she met them at the door.

Accepting the woman's warm hug, Rosaleen noticed the same scent of verbena she remembered from her first day in the doctor's office.

"I'm so glad Jacob succeeded in convincing you to come for a visit," the doctor's wife said as she took Jacob's hat and Rosaleen's bonnet before ushering them into the parlor.

Far smaller than the one at Opal Buchanan's boardinghouse, the Morgans' little parlor seemed cozy and inviting. The leaves of a large maple in the side yard dappled the afternoon sun onto the rose-patterned carpet. An early summer breeze fluttered the lace curtains at the tall, narrow open window.

Rosaleen's gaze roamed the room until it fixed on an object between the window and hearth. Suddenly, she felt her heart leap and her fingers itch. All other thoughts were swept away at the sight of the square piano.

"Rosaleen, do you play the piano? Rosaleen?"

"Yes," Rosaleen finally answered Becky Morgan's question with a breathless whisper. "I learned while employed at Mrs.

Griswold's Academy for Young Ladies in Jackson, Mississippi. Mrs. Griswold insisted that every girl under her roof learn at least the basic skills and social graces." Rosaleen experienced a bittersweet pang, remembering how her natural talent for the instrument had won her teacher's praise but scorn from the woman's other students. She turned a wobbly smile toward Becky. "I loved playing and discovered I have a talent for it."

Beaming, Jacob's sister clapped her hands. "Wonderful! Perhaps after refreshments we could prevail upon you to play something."

Offered the one temptation she could not resist, Rosaleen's desire for an abbreviated visit vanished. She felt herself being pulled deeper into the world of Madison—deeper into the world of Jacob Hale.

❧

As his sister served them lemon cake and tea, Jacob had to admit the afternoon outing had not been entirely unselfish on his part. Beyond the joy he derived from spending time in Rosaleen's company, he'd hoped to learn more about the beauty who'd wrapped her lovely fingers around his heart. And if he could grow their friendship, he might persuade her to attend worship services.

Now, something as unexpected as his sister's new piano promised a glimpse into Rosaleen Archer's carefully guarded past. Becky's request for her to play the piano had lit Rosaleen's eyes with a brightness Jacob had never seen in them. At his sister's urging, Rosaleen reminded him of a filly prancing in its carriage traces, eager to be off. As she was already on her feet, he suspected he'd have to physically restrain her in order to keep her from the piano.

For the better part of an hour, Jacob sat enthralled while Rosaleen worked through Becky's stack of sheet music, treating them to one beautiful piano piece after another. His sister's parlor rang with ballads and sonnets, as well as classical pieces.

The afternoon sun shimmered copper lights over Rosaleen's

lovely dark auburn tresses as she swayed with the melodies. Her eyes closed, her features held a beautiful tranquility. Somewhere in the midst of Beethoven's "Ode to Joy," Jacob knew he'd lost his heart.

Later that afternoon, as he strolled with Rosaleen along the streets of Madison, Jacob tried to keep his heart in check. He was still reeling from the discovery of her musical talent. *What other wondrous facets of this intriguing woman remain to be disclosed?*

"It's as beautiful as the finest plantation houses in Mississippi." Rosaleen's words jerked Jacob from his musings to the new home of railroad baron and financier, J. F. D. Lanier. She'd stopped their trek along High Street to admire the west side of the mansion with its brick facade painted light ocher brown.

"Yes, it's quite spectacular." He turned his attention to the grandiose example of Greek Revival architecture. Two white pillars supported a rather modest northern entrance, while at the south side four gigantic white pillars graced an expansive portico. Beyond that, a manicured lawn and garden swept down to the banks of the Ohio River.

"I'm sure I'll have to wait until I get to heaven for my mansion." His chuckle died at her somber demeanor. "Rosaleen, why do you avoid Sunday services? You should pay no attention to Opal's critiques of my sermons, you know." His attempt to inject levity failed to bring a smile to her face.

"I just don't think. . .I don't think it would do me any good."

"Why do you keep saying that? Have you read the scriptures at all?" An urgency to reach her caused frustration to rise within him.

"A little."

"But you don't think they pertain to you in any way?"

"No."

"How could you think that? The scriptures are for everyone."

"Reverend Hale!" Roscoe Stinnett's booming voice shoved its way into their conversation. "How are you on this fine May afternoon?"

Groaning inwardly, Jacob pasted a smile across his face. He preferred to believe that the quality of his sermons were the reason the president of Riverfront Porkpacking chose to attend his fledgling congregation. However, he suspected that was not the case.

In the midst of Madison's burgeoning industrialization, the forty-five-year-old Stinnett seemed determined to position himself as one of the town's fathers. Being a charter member of a new congregation could only elevate his standing in the community.

"I am quite well, Mr. Stinnett, thank you very much. Mrs. Archer and I were just admiring Mr. Lanier's new home."

A prickle of irritation marched up Jacob's neck when Stinnett afforded Rosaleen only a cursory nod. Jacob knew the man considered her an underling because she worked as a housemaid.

"Nice piece of architecture I suppose, though far too pretentious for my taste." Roscoe placed one hand over the other on the gold knob of his white walking cane and gave the financier's opulent abode little more than a glance. His haughty tone and dismissive attitude did nothing to hide the envy on the man's face. Jacob didn't doubt for a minute that Roscoe Stinnett would have a home twice the size of Lanier's if he could afford it.

Roscoe's tone and countenance brightened. "It is very fortuitous that we should have met this afternoon, Reverend Hale. My good wife and I have, only today, decided to make a considerable donation to the new church."

"That's very generous of you. I have opened an account at the bank, so you could simply—"

"No, no, my dear boy!" Stinnett's laugh shot through Jacob, causing his teeth to grind as his jaws tightened. "The donation is a piano. A Chickering square from Boston. Full cast-iron frame, new overstring design, all the rage, don't you know. Should arrive within the month."

Jacob felt Rosaleen's fingers grip his arm. His heart soared.

A piano might be just the enticement needed to get her to services.

No one else will be able to play as well as. . .

"That is but part of our donation. Myrtle has graciously agreed to be pianist."

"I—I don't know what to say." Truer words could not have come out of Jacob's mouth.

"Just doing our part, Reverend. Of course there will be a modest plaque affixed to the instrument, denoting Myrtle and I as the donors." Stinnett puffed out his chest, causing Jacob to fear the brass buttons might pop off the man's robin's-egg blue broadcloth coat.

"Thank you, Mr. Stinnett, and thank your good wife." Jacob watched Roscoe Stinnett saunter away, and the hope that had sprung briefly in his chest withered. He was glad for the new piano. Not only for the congregation, but so Rosaleen would have daily access to the instrument she loved. Yet what a perfect opportunity it would have been if she could have played for services and thus heard the Word proclaimed.

I trust You, Lord. I thank You for this and pray that in some way You will use this to bring Rosaleen to You.

six

"Never saw a man so eager to work that he plumb forgets to eat." Mrs. Buchanan smiled and shook her head.

Rosaleen watched Opal nestle a bottle of sweet tea and two tin cups into a basket, alongside freshly baked bread, fried chicken, and apple pie. Her large hands worked deftly, carefully tucking linen towels around the food.

Rosaleen chucked two pieces of wood into the Resor cookstove and chose not to be drawn into a conversation about Jacob Hale. After their afternoon outing the week before, she'd had enough trouble keeping the minister off her mind.

And Jacob Hale did unsettling things to her heart. His smile, his laugh, the sweet tenor of his voice, all set her heart dancing. She remembered the way his blue eyes had sparkled with appreciation at her piano playing...

No, I must not allow myself to get too close.

"Rosaleen, would you please take this basket down to Jacob and Andrew?" Opal straightened to her full height of nearly six feet and pushed back a strand of graying blond hair that had escaped from the bun at the back of her head. "With four new boarders, I have a million things to do, and Patsey will not be coming until this afternoon."

Feeling the familiar clash of emotions, Rosaleen closed the stove door with a *clang* and turned toward the kitchen table. "Of course."

Jacob Hale was a boarder, and her job as hired girl was to tend to the boarders. She brushed her hands on her calico apron and wished she could stifle the gladness bubbling up inside her at the thought of seeing him.

"You tell the fine young reverend that if he doesn't get

himself back here in time for supper, he'll get a right smart sermon from me."

Rosaleen only grinned at Opal's poor attempt at a stern face.

Outside, she inhaled deeply. The delicious smells of the bread, chicken, and apple pie blended with the pungent herbs growing in Opal's garden. Hollyhocks reclined against the white picket fence. Their bright pink flowers alive with the constant buzz of honeybees added to the cornucopia of fragrances.

As she headed up Mulberry toward Main-Cross Street, Rosaleen experienced a stab of sadness. She almost wished she could stay in Madison. On such a beautiful early June day, it was easy to believe she might actually blend into the population of the little river town.

As she walked the three blocks west on Main-Cross, she noticed fewer curious glances from the townspeople. It seemed most folks had become aware that she was Mrs. Buchanan's new hired girl.

Cool river breezes caressed her face when she turned south on Broadway Street. There, the downward grade of the street became steeper. She slowed her steps the final block to the building site of the church at the corner of Broadway and Second.

If only I could stay. If only I could have a future here with. . .

Rosaleen blinked away tears, unable to finish the thought. She looked down toward the Ohio, teeming with a flotilla of all shapes and sizes. Barges, ferries, and flatboats dotted the busy waterway.

The deep, breathy whistle of a steamboat wafted up from the river, sending a chill through her body. It reminded her of why she couldn't stay. Bill McGurty might be out there, lurking, ready to pounce like the predatory animal he was.

No, she couldn't stay. The moment she'd set aside enough money, she must leave for New York.

The ring of a hammer calmed her fears. Jacob was close by.

The thought sent her heart skipping.

There is no future for me here in Madison, especially with a preacher, she scolded her errant heart. It paid no heed, quickening even more when the smell of freshly cut lumber reached her nostrils and the building site came into view.

Jacob rose from pounding a wooden peg into a floorboard. "Hallo," he called with a wave of his hand, a smile stretching his handsome mouth.

She thought he looked a bit disconcerted as he walked toward her, brushing sawdust from his white linen work shirt and black trousers. Returning his smile, she raised the basket. "Opal sent me with your lunch."

"Mrs. Buchanan is of the opinion that if left to my own devices, I'd starve to death." Lifting the cloth for a peek inside the basket, he sniffed its contents. "Mmm. I'm not so sure she's wrong," he said with a chuckle, taking the basket from her hand.

A thoughtful look knitted his blond brows together. "Andrew and the three other men who've been helping me today have gone home for dinner. As Mrs. Buchanan seems to have sent enough for about three people, I'd be more than happy if you'd stay and share the repast with me. It could be a picnic."

A pang of guilt caused her to glance up Broadway. She really should be getting back. Her guilt evaporated in the warmth of his hopeful smile. "Yes, I'd like that." Disregarding her sternest admonition, Rosaleen's heart leaped when he took her hand in his.

He led her toward a whitewashed bench in the shade of a willow tree. Settling the basket on the bench between them, he handed her one of the two linen napkins then said a short prayer of thanks over the basket of food.

Rosaleen spent the uncomfortable moment watching men unload barrels from a flatboat. Prayers were for people like Jacob—people of whom God approved.

"I hope dining in the proximity of my friend's resting place does not offend you." A look of unease flitted across his face as he glanced at the nearby gravestone.

"No, not at all." She followed his gaze to the granite slab beneath the willow. Noticing the date on the marker, Rosaleen realized the grave was not an old one. "You were close to Mr. Whitaker, then?" She handed him a piece of buttered bread.

"Yes." He smiled down at the gravestone. "He was the circuit preacher who ministered to my home village. I'm afraid I was a bit of a scamp as a boy—got into a scrape or two." He grinned around a bite of the bread. "Along with my parents, Orville never gave up on me. One Sunday when I was nineteen, he preached a sermon from the book of Acts, the account of Peter preaching on the Day of Pentecost."

He paused to uncork the bottle of tea and pour them each a cup of the amber liquid. "I'd read that scripture many times. But somehow, that day, it spoke to my heart. I knew I'd come to a fork in the road and must either turn away from God's Word altogether or embrace it completely." Again, his face turned toward Reverend Whitaker's grave marker. "Thanks to Orville and my good Christian parents, I chose the latter."

Rosaleen had no knowledge of the scripture Jacob cited. What few sermons she'd heard her guardian preach had been thunderous admonitions from the Old Testament. She'd found no comfort in Wilfred Maguire's sermons.

"Was it then that you became a minister?"

"Yes. I began riding the circuit with Orville while he patiently taught me the deeper truths of the scriptures. Passages I'd read but never fully comprehended." His voice lowered. "Orville opened my heart to Christ's message of love." A pensive frown cleft his forehead, and he looked down at his dusty boot tops crossed at his ankles. "I only pray I might approach his deep understanding of the scriptures as well as his persuasive oratory."

His gaze shifted to the foundation and open floor of what would be the church. The distant look in his eyes suggested that he saw far beyond the bare beginnings to the finished building. "It will be beautiful, a fitting legacy to Orville. Especially after Andrew bricks it and we hang the bell."

He gave a quick wave of his hand, his voice sounding almost apologetic. "Oh, I know it sounds a bit boastful. Not all churches in Madison have bells. But I've been saving money for a five-hundred-pounder. According to the Verdin Bell Company of Cincinnati, it will cost a hundred dollars, but I'm determined to have it. At present, I've saved almost half the amount." His fists clenched, flexing his arm muscles. "I can almost feel the bell's glorious weight tugging against the rope in my hands as I ring it for the first time, inviting all within earshot to come and worship Christ."

Suddenly, he turned to face her, his blue gaze searching hers. "You were not taught the scriptures from childhood, were you?"

"No," Rosaleen murmured, glancing down at the cup of tea in her hands. She'd been content to sit and eat quietly as Jacob imparted bits of his past and future plans for the church. Now, she took a sip of sweet tea, wishing his quiet deduction hadn't felt so much like an accusation.

"I know nothing about you except that you worked at a young ladies' academy and play the piano like an angel. I'd like to know more, if you don't mind my asking. I'm afraid I'm a curious sort." With a disarming smile, he leaned back on the bench and began munching on a chicken leg.

Rosaleen felt her inhibitions melt at Jacob's caring tone. He might as well learn of her shameful heritage. Surely, then, he'd stop pestering her to attend his church services.

She looked down at the napkin in her lap, unwilling to watch disgust replace the kind expression on his face. The story began to tumble out like apples from a torn sack.

"I was raised until the age of twelve by my adoptive father, Rory Maguire. He was a gambler and the fourth son of an Irish earl. He met my mother, Rosie, a commoner, on the ship to New York from Ireland."

Rosaleen fidgeted, unfolding and refolding her napkin.

This was the part she most dreaded telling. "My mother was alone, single. . .and two months away from my arrival." She cast a wary glance toward Jacob. Finding no look of disgust or condemnation on his face encouraged her to continue.

A smile tugged at her lips. "Papa said he fell in love with my mother almost immediately. That she was sweet, full of life, and the most beautiful woman he'd ever seen."

"Then you must resemble her."

Rosaleen's heart hammered at Jacob's quiet comment. Disconcerted, she fixed her gaze on her hands twisting the piece of linen in her lap. "When they reached New York, Papa got my mother a decent apartment and asked her to be his wife. As a token of his intentions, he bought her the brooch you've seen me wear."

Jacob nodded. "Yes, I've noticed it. It's beautiful. He must have loved your mother very much."

Jacob's gentle tone caused a knot of tears to gather in her throat.

"They married, then?" Jacob asked before taking a big bite of chicken.

"No. One evening Papa came to my mother's place to let her know he'd found a domestic position for her as soon as she delivered her baby. He found her alone and in labor. Unable to find a midwife, Papa helped to bring me into the world. An hour later, my mother died." Rosaleen's voice drooped. Tears stung her eyes, and she wondered why she still wept over a mother she'd never known.

"Rosaleen, I'm so sorry—"

She waved off his condolences. "Before she died, my mother begged Papa to take me and raise me as his own. And so he did." Her voice lifted with her spirit at the memory.

"We traveled the steamboats up and down the Mississippi, Missouri, and Ohio Rivers—wherever the next card game presented itself. Papa provided me a happy and interesting childhood, although many times we barely had enough money to get by. I'm afraid my father, though a persistent gambler, was not a very successful one."

"Then you've never had a real home?" For the first time, she caught a glimpse of concern flit across his face.

She shook her head and took a sip of sweet tea. "No, but never having had one, I didn't miss it."

"Is that why your father sent you to the young ladies' academy—so you'd have a home?" He pitched the chicken bone to the grassy slope where a pair of blackbirds set upon it, noisily feuding over the prize.

"No. My father became ill." She fought new tears and somehow managed the hateful word, "Consumption. I was but twelve and he didn't want to leave me alone. His older brother and wife, from whom he'd been estranged for many years, live in Natchez, Mississippi. They reluctantly agreed to take me but found my illegitimacy unacceptable. Within a month, they sent me to Jackson, Mississippi, and into Mrs. Griswold's employ as a housemaid."

Her voice lowered, and she winced at the recollection. "Six months later, I learned of my father's death."

"Rosaleen, I'm sorry. I never meant to resurrect such painful memories."

The sweetness of Jacob's voice and his hand covering hers sent more tears sketching down her cheeks.

"Sooo," Jacob stretched out the word, "where does Mr. Archer come in?"

She drew in a shaky breath and continued. "August of last year, Mrs. Griswold's academy closed, and I returned to my guardian's home." Her lips twitched with a tiny, forced smile. "The moment I arrived, I was informed I'd be marrying Mr. Donovan Archer, a riverboat pilot thirteen years my senior." Rosaleen turned the thin gold band on the third finger of her left hand. Thoughts of her late husband always brought a rush of fond memories, and she smiled. "Donovan was looking for a wife familiar with life on the river."

"Then you and Mr. Archer weren't—I mean there hadn't been a courtship—I mean. . ."

Rosaleen hurried to Jacob's rescue when he stumbled for an appropriate description of her unexpected union. "It was a marriage of convenience. Mr. Archer was a widower of some years and a kind and honorable man." She met Jacob's intent gaze and hoped he could discern from her look the sentiment of love lacking in her brief marriage. She also hoped to convey the mutual respect and caring that had defined it.

"I'm sure he was," Jacob replied. "I'm so sorry to learn of the grief you've experienced but glad God sent you a season of joy, however brief."

While they finished the two pieces of apple pie in silence, Rosaleen found it impossible to read the thoughts behind his eyes.

Suddenly, he leaned toward her and took her hands into his, causing her to emit a soft gasp of surprise. The comfort of his strong, warm grasp filled Rosaleen with longing. She could only imagine how wonderful it might feel to be enveloped in the sanctuary of his arms, to rest her head against his chest.

"Rosaleen, you are young. God has so many wonderful things waiting for you, if you will only allow Him to guide you."

Her gaze followed his to the building under construction.

"I realize it doesn't look like much now, but God willing, by winter, I will be the pastor of a fine church and growing congregation. A congregation that could be the family you've been denied. I pray that you might allow me to be a part—"

"Jacob!" The man's shouted greeting and the mule-drawn wagon rattling to a stop on Broadway broke into Jacob's entreaty. "We got that load of two-by-eights from the lumber yard."

Heart pounding, Rosaleen stood and hastily covered the remnants of their lunch with the linen cloths. What had he been about to suggest? She told herself that she was thankful their conversation had been brought to an abrupt close. She attempted a light tone but couldn't keep the tremor from her voice. "Mrs. Buchanan will be wondering what's keeping me."

Jacob sent a quick glance of dismay toward the three men

unloading the lumber from the wagon. As he caught her arm in a gentle grasp, his gaze searched hers. "Please, just consider the possibility of my suggestion."

Rosaleen nodded, amazed that he'd still want anything to do with her after what he'd learned. She hurried toward Broadway, the graveled street blurring through her tears. What must he think of her? She'd told too much. She was glad she'd stopped short of confessing the horrors she'd experienced at the hands of Bill McGurty.

He meant nothing more than wanting me to attend his church, that's all.

Whether she believed that made little difference. She knew it was best if she did believe it.

Three blasts of a steamboat's whistle shot fear through her, and she quickened her steps. She must leave Madison at the earliest possible moment.

As difficult as it might be to accomplish that task, it would be simple compared to the impossibility of expunging Jacob Hale from her heart.

seven

Jacob sat in a horsehair-upholstered wing chair, his face aching from the smile he'd pasted across it. He found only marginal consolation in the fact that the faces of every other person in the parlor mirrored his own.

Broken only by the occasional wince, the stiff features of his congregation expressed their mutual suffering.

Seeming oblivious to the torture she was inflicting, Myrtle Stinnett sat before the keyboard of the new piano, butchering "Rock of Ages."

Before the final note of the hymn had mercifully faded away, Jacob jumped to his feet. "Thank you so very much, Mrs. Stinnett, for that moving rendition."

He hurried to help her up from the piano bench, fearing she might be inspired to deliver an encore. After leading the congregation in benediction, he wrestled with the thorny problem as he mingled with his flock.

The new piano, which had arrived earlier in the week, had indeed proved a mixed blessing. His heart sang remembering the joy that lit Rosaleen's face as workers uncrated it in the parlor. A near twin to Becky and Ephraim's instrument, it now graced the front left quadrant of the room.

Later that day, he'd caught Rosaleen walking around the piano. Watching her fingers stroking the beautiful rosewood finish of the cabinet, he'd begged her to play something from the complimentary sheet music the manufacturer had sent along with the instrument.

For the next half hour, he and Mrs. Buchanan, along with Andrew and Patsey Chapman, sat enthralled, listening to a hauntingly beautiful rendition of Beethoven's "Moonlight Sonata."

Frustration gripped Jacob as he left the parlor to bid his parishioners good day at the front door. Shaking hands absently, he prayed for God's intervention. *Lord, somehow You must help me find a way to replace Myrtle Stinnett with Rosaleen as pianist for worship services.* Psalm 27:14 sprang to his mind. "*Wait on the LORD: be of good courage, and he shall strengthen thine heart: wait, I say, on the LORD.*"

"Well, Reverend Hale, do you not agree that the new piano is a wonderful addition to services, especially with Myrtle at the keyboard?"

Roscoe Stinnett's question jerked Jacob from his reverie. Except for his sister, Becky, and her family, the Stinnetts were the last in the line of parishioners filing out of the boardinghouse.

Praying for guidance, Jacob chose his words carefully. "I do believe it shall prove to be a true blessing. Again, I thank you and Mrs. Stinnett for your generosity."

He turned his attention to Myrtle Stinnett's slight, retiring figure, half hidden behind her husband's robust bulk. Her reticent demeanor beside her overbearing husband always evoked a feeling of sympathy from Jacob. "As for your contribution as pianist, Mrs. Stinnett, I'm speechless."

"My playing would have been better if my rheumatism wasn't acting up," she murmured, her eyes not quite meeting his. Grimacing, she wrung her lace-gloved hands then lowered her pinched features until they disappeared behind her gray bonnet.

Loath to injure the shy woman's feelings, Jacob said, "I can honestly say, I found it unequalled by anything I've heard before."

A satisfied smile settled across Roscoe Stinnett's broad face. He made their farewells and guided his wife outside to join others of the congregation visiting on the lawn.

"Jacob."

Jacob turned at his sister's urgent whisper.

"Is there nothing you can do?"

"I only wish there were, Becky." He gave a wistful sigh and reached out and touched the soft, rosy cheek of his infant niece cooing in her mother's arms. "The sad thing is, I feel sure it was not Myrtle's idea to act as pianist but Roscoe's."

"Yes," Becky agreed, repositioning the ivory crocheted wrap the baby had kicked off. "I'm afraid the man bullies her. But you know Myrtle, she'd never say boo to a goose. If only—"

"I know," he finished her thought, "if only Rosaleen could play for services."

"Perhaps I can help." Ephraim, with Daniel in hand, joined his wife. "I confess I was tempted to accompany Daniel on his last trip to the outhouse."

"But what could you do, dear?" Becky asked.

Jacob, too, wondered what his brother-in-law had in mind.

"I'm not altogether sure, but a few prayers concerning the subject would not be misplaced this week," Ephraim told them, grinning.

As Jacob watched his sister and her family walk away, he prayed that God had given Ephraim a solution to their prickly problem. Now, if only he could convince Rosaleen to attend services.

Jacob stood at the front door shaking hands, eager to see the last parishioner from the boardinghouse. He continually cast glances down the hallway toward the kitchen where he'd last glimpsed Rosaleen.

Since the day last week when she'd disclosed her history, he'd found his course set and his heart determined. Somehow he must bring her to the knowledge of Christ's love and salvation.

The moment he bid the last straggler good day, Jacob noticed Rosaleen heading toward the stairway with an armful of linens.

He bolted toward her. "Rosaleen"—touching her arm, he halted her ascent at the bottom step—"I saw you listening during the services. . .out in the hallway."

"I—"

"Don't deny it." He couldn't help giving her a little grin. "I was wondering if you'd consider playing for Sunday services."

"But you have a pianist. I heard—"

"Then you realize just how desperately we require your assistance." Jacob widened his grin.

"But, I'm not—I mean I don't belong. . ."

The way her gaze dropped to the linens ripped at his heart. How could she not realize how talented, beautiful, and wonderful she was?

"But you do belong. You are exactly who belongs there." Lifting her chin with the crook of his finger, Jacob forced her to meet his intent gaze. "Rosaleen, you have an amazing talent. If you heard some of my sermon today, you know it dealt with the parable of the talents from the book of Matthew. God gave you this talent. Could you not give just a little of it back?"

He watched her delicate brows slant into a V. "Jacob, I wouldn't want to cause problems between you and your congregation."

Though her concern touched him deeply, his heart lifted, detecting a tiny crack in her resistance. He rushed to take advantage of the opportunity, however slight. "Would you take the position if it were open?"

She caught her bottom lip with her teeth, and then after a moment's hesitation, murmured, "Yes."

Jacob felt himself exhale a breath he hadn't realized he'd been holding. "Don't be concerned about injuring Myrtle Stinnett's feelings," he told her. "I am quite sure she would like to relinquish the position as much as the congregation would like for her to. I'm also confident that the good lady has other talents far more obvious than those musical."

❧

The following Wednesday afternoon, Jacob sat at the desk in the parlor, immersed in preparation for the next Sunday's sermon.

Suddenly, Rosaleen's soft voice pulled his attention toward the doorway. "Jacob."

As always, Jacob's heart quickened at her presence.

"Mrs. Stinnett is waiting in the front hallway and wonders if she could have a few minutes of your time."

"Yes, of course, Rosaleen. Please show her in."

Jacob's mind raced, trying to imagine what the woman might want. He found himself unprepared for the sight of Myrtle Stinnett dabbing at her eyes with a lace kerchief.

Hurrying to the distraught woman's side, he gently ushered her to the green velvet upholstered settee. "My dear lady, whatever could be the problem?"

After situating Mrs. Stinnett, he turned to Rosaleen. "Rosaleen, would you please bring Mrs. Stinnett a cup of tea and some of Patsey's little seed cakes?"

"Yes, of course," Rosaleen said, hurrying toward the kitchen.

"Please tell me, Mrs. Stinnett, what has so distressed you?" Jacob pulled the white and yellow silk-upholstered armchair nearer to the settee.

Seeming to have collected herself to some degree, Myrtle Stinnett winced as she twisted the lace kerchief in her lap. "I am sorry to have to inform you, Reverend, but I can no longer act as pianist for the congregation."

"And why would that be, Mrs. Stinnett?" Inwardly rejoicing, Jacob knew he must walk a very fine line. Surely no one would have been so discourteous as to have commented on her lack of musical ability. Careful not to suggest any such thing, he simply waited for her response.

"I had an appointment this morning with your kinsman, Dr. Morgan." She glanced down at her gloved hands folded in her lap. "It's my hands, you see."

"Your hands?"

"Yes. As I mentioned to you after services last Sunday, I suffer from rheumatism. My hands have been hurting worse than ever, and Dr. Morgan suggested that playing the piano for services may further aggravate the inflammation." With her left hand, she rubbed the knuckles of her right.

"I know this leaves you without a pianist, and I know

Roscoe, too, will be so disappointed. . . ." Her words broke on a soft sob. She dabbed again at her eyes. "But it seems to be either that or my sewing, and I simply will *not* abandon my needlework."

"No, no, of course you mustn't." Jacob reached over to pat her hand, his heart going out to the woman. "I'm sure someone will step forward and fill the void."

Suddenly she sat straight up, a flash of inspiration registering on her face. "I nearly forgot. My niece, Sophie, will be arriving next week from Miss Ely's Young Ladies' Academy in Cincinnati. She has undoubtedly mastered the piano. Why, you must know her—Sophie Schuler? She hails from your home village up in Hamilton County."

"Sophie Schuler is your niece?" Stunned by the revelation, Jacob barely noticed Rosaleen enter with the tea and cakes.

"Why, yes. When Sophie was born, I promised my sister, Gerite, Sophie's mother, that Roscoe and I would see to her formal schooling." Murmuring a thank-you to Rosaleen, Myrtle accepted the offered tea. After pausing to take a sip, she chatted on about how she planned to bring Sophie into Madison's social circle and hoped to persuade her niece to make Madison her permanent home.

Allowing the woman to prattle on uninterrupted, Jacob found his mind flashing back to his earlier acquaintance with the young Miss Schuler. He'd known Sophie since she was a child. Two years ago, while spending a summer with his brother's family, he'd briefly courted the then seventeen-year-old Sophie. However, at that time, he'd felt the seven-year age difference too great, and they'd gone their separate ways—him to Madison and her to. . .*her to a young ladies' academy*.

"Oh Reverend, I feel so much better." Brightening, Myrtle Stinnett nibbled on a seed cake, her attitude much revived. "Of course Sophie can play the piano!"

Jacob's heart slumped with his shoulders.

Oh Lord, help me. What am I to do now?

eight

"Wonder what the reverend thinks 'bout his ole flame comin' to spend the summer in Madison?" Patsey asked as she cut out biscuits at the kitchen table.

At Patsey's giggled question, Rosaleen's gaze jerked up from the strips of bacon sizzling in the frying pan. She wondered whom Patsey could mean.

The housemaid's next words supplied the answer. "Yes sirree, wish I could'a been in the parlor when Mrs. Stinnett told him who her niece is! I can jist imagine the look on his face."

A sharp glance from Opal shushed Patsey, drying up her chuckle.

Patsey's inadvertent disclosure only added to Rosaleen's discomfort when an hour later, sitting beside the piano among a parlor full of worshipers, she found herself in the last place she'd wanted to be.

Rosaleen had been prepared to dislike Sophie Schuler, but she couldn't. Throughout the service, she'd found her attention drawn to the girl.

Her heart wilting, Rosaleen was forced to admit that the young woman would be a perfect match for Jacob. Her honey blond hair peeking from beneath her rose-studded bonnet matched his almost exactly. Her pale blue eyes were but a few shades lighter than his.

Squished between her aunt and uncle on the black horsehair sofa, the quiet, petite young woman seemed the picture of demure grace. Sophie's carefully fashioned side curls framed her face in gold ringlets. With the slightest movement, they brushed against her alabaster cheek that bloomed the pale pink of wild roses. Mostly, the Stinnetts' niece kept her gaze fixed on her white-gloved hands, clasped in the lap of her rose taffeta skirt. Occasionally, however, she'd cast a shy glance up toward Jacob, who stood preaching from the open Bible draped across his outstretched arm.

From her vantage point beside the piano, Rosaleen squirmed on the gold velvet-upholstered hassock. She wondered if anyone was actually listening to Jacob's sermon, as all eyes seemed trained on either Sophie Schuler or herself.

Lacing her fingers together, she pressed her balled fists into the lap of her blue chintz dress. Self-conscious, she felt sure everyone would recognize it as one of Becky Morgan's cast-offs.

After the initial butterflies in her stomach settled down, she'd actually enjoyed playing for the service. Jacob's introduction had been mercifully brief and simple, describing her as "Mrs. Archer, an accomplished pianist in Mrs. Buchanan's employ, who'll be filling in at the piano for a time."

Also, she'd been surprised to find herself enjoying watching him preach. What she heard bore scarce resemblance to the fire-and-brimstone sermons her former guardian had leveled at his congregation. Jacob's voice, tender and moving, spoke of God's enduring love and His calling of all to repentance.

All!

Jacob's impassioned but gentle voice reading the words of Jesus brought tears to her eyes. Could it actually mean what it said? Could it mean her?

She found the picture Jacob painted of Christ as the Good Shepherd a compelling one. One she longed to grasp. Yet she could still hear Wilfred Maguire's contradicting words ringing in her ears.

"You are a harlot's spawn—wicked and irredeemable."

It was all so confusing. Which was right? Which was wrong? Rosaleen didn't think she could bear opening her heart, hoping to find inclusion, only to learn that Jesus' invitation did not apply to her and that her former guardian had been right.

She looked at Jacob then at Sophie Schuler. One way or

another, her heart seemed destined to be broken in Madison, Indiana.

At the conclusion of Jacob's sermon, Rosaleen watched for his nod. Taking her place at the piano, she accompanied the congregation in their singing of "Blest Be the Tie That Binds."

During the benediction, she sat quietly, feeling very apart from the others in the room. Did God actually hear Jacob's heartfelt words? Would he hear hers? The last time she remembered expressing anything that resembled a prayer had been that night in the river when she'd feared drowning. Had God heard her? Had it been His hand that saved her?

"Rosaleen."

Jacob's voice startled her from her musings, and she whirled around on the piano seat. Rosaleen hated the jealousy gripping her as Jacob approached arm in arm with Sophie Schuler.

"Rosaleen, there is someone I'd like you to meet." He smiled, glancing affectionately at the diminutive blond girl beside him. "This is Sophie Schuler, an old friend from my home village."

Standing, Rosaleen smiled, surprised at how easy and genuine the response came.

"Sophie, this is Mrs. Rosaleen Archer. She has graciously agreed to act as pianist for our congregation until such a time as you might feel prepared to accept that duty."

"I—I don't know. Oh Jacob, must I?" Sophie murmured through her fingertips she pressed against her lips.

Rosaleen saw stark fear glisten in Sophie's pale blue eyes.

"Why, no. Of course you don't have to if you'd rather not."

As Jacob patted Sophie's hand, Rosaleen felt a pain in the vicinity of her heart.

"Mrs. Archer is such a wonderful pianist. I'm afraid the piano was not one of the studies at which I excelled during my education at Miss Ely's Academy for Girls. Would you mind terribly continuing your music ministry, Mrs. Archer?" Hope shone from the girl's eyes.

At once, Rosaleen felt both ashamed of her own jealousy and compelled to relieve the girl's anxiety. "No, of course not."

Glancing at Jacob, Rosaleen experienced a flash of irritation when she saw him fight a grin. She realized he was reacting to Sophie's suggestion that her piano playing was some sort of "ministry."

"Like my Aunt Myrtle, I'd much rather do needlework," Sophie admitted. "But I do dread telling Uncle Roscoe. He's already out of sorts because I spend so much time with Edith Applegate." She raised her chin in a defiant pose. "But Edith was my very best friend at Miss Ely's, and I can't help it if Uncle Roscoe is angry with her papa."

Rosaleen remembered Opal mentioning the falling out between Roscoe Stinnett and Edward Applegate. According to Opal, when Edward Applegate left Riverfront Porkpacking to start his own pork packing business, the two men became bitter rivals, undercutting one another at every turn.

"Why don't you leave your uncle to me," Jacob offered, to which Sophie responded with a grateful smile.

"Oh, thank you, Jacob." Sophie bounced like a giddy child. She glanced across the room where her aunt and uncle stood conversing with another couple. "Now, while Uncle Roscoe's attention is diverted, I must catch up with Edith and her brother, Edwin." Sophie murmured a quick good-bye, and with a rustling of her taffeta skirts, went to join a young lady with strawberry blond curls, standing beside a tall young man of the same coloring.

"She's a very sweet girl." Rosaleen meant every word as she followed Jacob's gaze across the room.

"Yes. Yes, she is." His soft voice held a thoughtful tone. As he turned his full attention to Rosaleen, his tone and countenance brightened. "I want to commend you on the wonderful job you did today. I'm sure my heart was not the only one touched by your playing." His mouth quirked in a mischievous grin. "Sophie was right. It is a ministry, you know."

Rosaleen stiffened. "I play the piano, that's all." Suggesting that someone God refused to recognize could perform any kind of ministry seemed beyond absurd. She wouldn't be forced to be something she wasn't—not ever again.

"Rosaleen"—her heart pranced when he gazed into her eyes and took her hands in his—"I know this was not the first sermon you've heard me preach. For the last couple of weeks, I've noticed you in the hallway outside the parlor door during worship services. You're searching for something, and you don't know what it is. But I do."

Reveling in the touch of his hands on hers, Rosaleen made no comment, unable to speak over the knot in her throat. She wished he'd never let go.

When his fingers slipped away, she felt bereft. She watched him walk to the mahogany desk near the parlor window and retrieve a small brown paper package.

"Please take this. It is in appreciation of your agreeing to play for services." He pressed the package into her hands, and his gaze melted into hers. "Please promise me you'll read it. If you have any questions, any at all, please ask me and I'll endeavor to help answer them."

Rosaleen managed a smile and a nod.

That night she sat cross-legged on her straw mattress, the Bible Jacob had given her in her lap. In the flickering light of the lantern hanging from the wall sconce, she read the words of Jesus. Her eyes misted as she read from Matthew 11:28–29: "Come unto me, all ye that labour and are heavy laden, and I will give you rest. Take my yoke upon you, and learn of me; for I am meek and lowly in heart: and ye shall find rest unto your souls."

Could Jesus give her peace? Could he accept a soul that had been a mistake?

All afternoon her heart had warred. Jacob had spent the day at the Stinnetts', visiting Sophie. Rosaleen knew she should be happy for him if he were to renew his relationship with the sweet Sophie. He deserved a pure, unblemished wife.

Tears seeped through her lashes as she shut her eyes tight

against the awful scenes flashing behind them: Bill McGurty's whiskey-laced breath hot on her face. Her useless struggles. Then there were the others—those Bill had sent to her in order to curry their favor. And those times he had forced her to steal what he hadn't taken from them at the gambling table.

Shame that no amount of tears could extinguish burned her face and twisted through her like a hot poker. Her heart crumbled beneath the weight of the disgusting memories, and she gave way to sobs.

Why had she ever allowed the thought to flit across her mind that Jacob Hale might ever care for her? She felt like a dirty rag beside Sophie Schuler's spotless purity.

Collapsing to the straw mattress, she pressed the Bible against her broken heart.

Oh Jesus, help me.

nine

The surprising aroma of baking bread met Rosaleen as she descended the stairs. Her curiosity growing, she glanced at the transom window above the front door. The first faint rays of dawn stained the glass pink. This was Tuesday. They always baked on Wednesday, but even then, they never began this early.

Since her arrival at the boardinghouse, one of Rosaleen's jobs had been to start the cookstove each morning. Confused, she quickened her steps, worried that Mrs. Buchanan might consider her negligent in her duties.

Just outside the kitchen door, she stopped short, her bewilderment compounding when she saw Patsey Chapman, who never came before seven in the morning.

"Patsey, what are you doing here so early?" Rosaleen snatched her apron off the peg behind the door, deciding Opal must have forgotten to mention to her they'd be baking early this morning.

At Rosaleen's exclamation, Patsey turned from the open oven door and pressed her finger to her lips. "Shh. Don't want to wake up the whole house yet."

Rosaleen lowered her voice to just above a whisper. "Why are we making bread on Tuesday, and so early? Opal never said anything to me about it."

Hampered by her expanded middle, Patsey groaned as she bent over and pulled another loaf of freshly baked bread from the oven. "Gonna have more mouths to feed in a day or two—lots more."

Still confused, Rosaleen shook her head. "Mrs. Buchanan never mentioned anything about more boarders."

Patsey lowered her voice, her bright eyes darting about as

if concerned that someone else might be listening. "Not for here. For Georgetown." She shoved another loaf of bread dough into the oven. "Andrew jis got word yesterday. There's a train a-comin'."

"Runaways?" Rosaleen blurted, forgetting to whisper.

"Shh!" Patsey's brow furrowed, and she shot a nervous glance through the kitchen window into the half-lit, dewy garden. Even the mention of the word aloud infused her face with fear. She supplied further information in a quick, staccato whisper. "Andrew got word. Don't know when. Jis got to be ready."

"Good morning, Patsey. Rosaleen." Smiling, Opal walked into the kitchen tying on her apron. Her demeanor gave no indication that she found anything at all odd about baking bread at the crack of dawn on a Tuesday. She dipped water from the bucket by the door into the teakettle and set it on top of the stove.

"Patsey, you know that big ham hanging near the door of the smokehouse?" At Patsey's nod, Opal continued in a conversational tone. "Well, I'm afraid it might go bad in this heat, so if you know people who could use it, have Andrew take it to your place this evening, would you?"

"Yes'm."

Rosaleen listened to Patsey's muted reply and scooped flour into a large crockery bowl from a muslin sack. Suddenly, she realized Opal, too, knew about the expected arrival of the runaways. Feeling a kinship with those running from oppression, Rosaleen turned to Mrs. Buchanan. "Is there anything I can do to help, Opal?"

Opal pinned her with a knowing stare, but her tone remained light and unconcerned. "Why, of course, Rosaleen. This is a boardinghouse," she said with a little chuckle. "There's always something to do."

Nodding, Rosaleen understood. She must make no mention of the Underground Railroad.

Opal turned her attention to cutting thick slices of bacon

that she then laid in the sizzling-hot cast-iron frying pan. "Reverend Hale left before dawn to work on that church building again. That man's gonna keel over if he keeps workin' hours on end without eatin'. Rosaleen, I'd like for you to take him this bacon with some of Patsey's good bread and a little jug of milk."

Rosaleen jerked her head up from the bread dough she'd begun kneading at the kitchen table. Her mind raced with her heart. Feeling sure he'd renewed his relationship with Sophie Schuler, Rosaleen had vowed to spend as little time in Jacob's presence as possible. "But shouldn't I help Patsey—"

"Patsey has things well in hand, and any assistance she might need, I can give her." Opal packed the bacon, bread, and jug of milk into a linen-lined basket.

A few minutes later, Rosaleen headed out the back door toward Main-Cross Street. She slowed her steps when she reached Broadway. The morning sun shining through the trees dappled the street with gold. Its warmth on her shoulders did nothing to brighten her heart. Perhaps she could simply hand him the basket and leave.

I'll tell him I have work to do at the boardinghouse, I'll say—

Her musings broke off as she neared the building site. The mule team hitched to a wagon of lumber stood tied and unattended, but she heard no ringing of a hammer or *whoosh* of a saw. Fear grabbed at her heart. Had he been hurt? Was he lying somewhere injured or. . . "Jacob! Jacob, where are you?"

"Rosaleen?"

A relieved sigh puffed from Rosaleen's lips when Jacob's blond head popped up from the far side of the building.

"Mmm, breakfast." Smiling, he hurried to her side and took the basket from her hand. He lifted the cloth, releasing the delicious smells of fresh-baked bread and fried bacon. Rosaleen's heart bucked when he set the basket on the ground and took her hand in his.

"I was hoping you'd come this morning." He gave her a mischievous grin. "I can always depend on Mrs. Buchanan's insistence that I eat breakfast."

Happiness bubbled up inside Rosaleen at knowing he'd expected her, had been waiting for her.

"Come, I want to show you something."

They rounded the church, now framed by skeletal walls of vertical two-by-fours. "There will be stone steps later," he said, helping her up the makeshift wooden steps into what would be the sanctuary.

She grasped his hand and her heart ached at his nearness. *If only—if only. . .*

Never in her life had she wanted to feel a man's arms around her more than at this moment.

"Here." Oblivious to her thoughts, he towed her to a sunny spot near the front of the church. Stepping behind her, he gently grasped her shoulders and turned her toward an opening in the wall at the east side of the sanctuary. "This is the spot where we'll put the piano—here by the window, where the morning sun will shine through."

The angle presented a nearly uncluttered view of the Ohio River, shimmering in the morning sunlight.

"This is what I want you to see each Sunday morning." His soft breath caressed her face as he bent his head over her shoulder.

Though she found the scene beautiful, it was the nearness of his face that took her breath away.

How easy it would be to lean my head against his neck, to turn my face ever so slightly. . . No! I mustn't do this, I mustn't!

Pulling away from his grasp, she turned and stepped backward. When her left foot found only air, she gasped, her right foot teetering on the edge of the floor.

Fear constricted her chest when she glanced down at a pile of bricks below. Suddenly, she felt Jacob's arms around her, pulling her back into the building and hard against him.

Wrapped in his strong arms, she surrendered to temptation, pressing her head against his chest. Her heart hammering, she clung to him. This was what she'd wanted. The moment she'd dreamed of for so long—to melt in the embrace of her angel's arms.

"Rosaleen," he murmured, sounding as breathless as she felt. The stubble of his unshaven chin prickled against her cheek as he nudged her face back. For a moment, their gaze held. Then, as his eyes closed and his face lowered, their lips met.

Feeling as limp as a rag doll, Rosaleen luxuriated in the kiss, glad that Jacob's strong arms supported her, holding her tight.

The sudden realization of what was happening jolted her from the beautiful trance. She pushed away from him, tears of regret stinging her eyes.

Rosaleen felt wretched. How could she do this to Sophie? Sweet, naive little Sophie. Jacob deserved better. He deserved someone like Sophie. "We—we mustn't." Filled with panic and disgust, she stumbled away from him toward the front steps.

"Rosaleen, I—I never meant. . ."

Disregarding the look of bewildered pain in his blue eyes, Rosaleen fled down the steps and ran sobbing across town until she reached the boardinghouse.

Trembling at the backyard pump, she washed the tears from her face. How could she have allowed such a thing to happen? Her heart sank at the awful truth.

Reverend Maguire was right. I am evil.

Her resolve stiffened. She must leave Madison as soon as possible.

Glad to find Opal and Patsey gone from the kitchen, Rosaleen headed for the stairs. Still shaking, she sought the solitude of her little attic room.

Just as her foot touched the first step, she heard a sharp rap at the front door. With a sigh, she trudged across the front hallway in no mood to greet new boarders with a cheerful smile.

She swung the door open and stood, stunned.

ten

"Alistair?" The name burst from Rosaleen's lips as she stood staring wide-eyed at Alistair "The Earl" Ralston.

She'd known the accomplished young thimblerigger and three-card-monte sharp most of her life. Continually moving from one riverboat to another, she and her father had crossed paths with Alistair many times.

The puzzled look on the man's face changed to joyful surprise as recognition flickered in his eyes. "Rosaleen? Rosaleen Maguire, is it really you?"

Rosaleen managed to nod.

He grinned, showing off his gold front tooth. "Well, as I live and breathe! If it ain't our own little Rosaleen, all growed up. Ain't ya gonna invite me in? That is, if you have a room to rent."

"Yes—yes, we do." Still reeling from the surprise, Rosaleen stepped aside to allow Alistair into the front hallway.

His gaze seemed to sweep the little hallway, taking in its gold and white patterned wallpaper, mahogany table with a pair of Aragon lamps, and floral ingrained carpet. "Not bad." He gave her a wink. "Nice as any of old Vanderbilt's steamboats." His grin faded, and he pulled his black beaver hat from his wavy auburn hair. His gray eyes held a look of genuine sympathy. "Heard about your dad sometime back. Real sorry. Heard you went to live with relations or somethin'."

"Something like that." She questioned the wisdom of telling Alistair too much. Had he learned of her time with Bill McGurty? If he had, he'd chosen to pretend otherwise. Alistair would know as well as anyone that few crossed Black Jack Bill McGurty and lived.

"Little Rosaleen." Smiling, he shook his head in disbelief. "You've grown into a beauty, and that's a fact." Though his gaze roved over her, it caused her no unease. His benign assessment of her seemed to convey only a brotherly pride.

Rosaleen had to admit that the six-foot-tall Alistair cut a handsome figure in his dark green broadcloth coat and black tapered trousers. He held out his arms. "How about a kiss for an old friend?"

Before she could protest, Alistair caught her up in a bay-rum-scented bear hug. Lifting her feet off the floor, he planted a wet kiss on her mouth.

"Rosaleen, I came as soon as I got the chance. We need to talk—" Jacob's voice coming from the hall doorway that led to the kitchen sounded winded.

As Alistair set her down, Rosaleen whirled in time to see Jacob's face go ashen then bright scarlet. Without another word, he turned on his heel and strode back toward the kitchen.

Alistair gave a nervous-sounding cough and cleared his throat. "Well, I don't want to keep you from your work, so if you'll just show me to my room. . ."

Humiliated, Rosaleen paid only vague attention to Alistair's words, her helpless gaze fixed on the spot where Jacob had stood.

What must Jacob think?

She'd allowed him to kiss her earlier, and now Jacob had witnessed Alistair stealing a kiss from her. With her heart feeling as leaden as her feet, she mounted the stairs with Ralston in tow. At the landing, she glanced down at the open parlor door and felt torn. She desperately wanted to explain to Jacob Alistair's meaningless kiss. But that would undoubtedly lead to a discussion of the kiss she and Jacob had shared—a far more troublesome topic.

That evening as everyone sat around the supper table, Jacob was uncharacteristically quiet. It struck Rosaleen that he seemed to go out of his way to avoid looking at her. However, he shot continual, scrutinizing glances toward Alistair.

Rosaleen was almost glad for Alistair's constant banter. The man had the gift of gab, but she made a mental note to count the silverware after supper.

"Never expected to find you working at a boardinghouse," Alistair said, smiling across the table at Rosaleen.

"Mrs. Archer is a wonderful help," Opal injected. "I'm truly blessed to have her."

"Archer?" Alistair's brows shot up then slipped down into a thoughtful V. "Ah yes, now that I think on it, I did hear something about Rory Maguire's girl marrying Donovan Archer."

Then turning quiet, he focused his attention on the large slice of ham on his plate. His sudden change of attitude made Rosaleen wonder if he'd also heard about Bill McGurty shooting Donovan to death.

Opal clucked her tongue and shook her head sadly. "Such an awful thing, Mr. Archer perishing in that steamboat explosion. We just thank the Lord Rosaleen was spared."

A look of surprise flashed across Alistair's face. "Real sorry to hear about Archer, Rosaleen. Good man from what I recall."

Rosaleen murmured her thanks. Although Alistair's surprise seemed genuine, she couldn't tell if it was from just now learning of her husband's death or because Opal's comment contradicted what Alistair might have heard about Donovan's murder.

She studied the gambler's features, but his face had gone poker plain, unreadable. If he did know the truth about how Donovan died and about her time with Bill McGurty, he didn't seem inclined to divulge that knowledge. And at the moment, that suited Rosaleen. As much as she would like to know if Alistair had seen Bill since the explosion, she would rather Opal and Jacob—especially Jacob—not learn of her time with Bill. So she was relieved when Opal steered the supper conversation in a different direction.

"I have to admit, Mr. Ralston," Opal said as she passed Alistair a plate of corn bread, "this is the first time I've had the privilege of entertaining an English earl at my dining table."

Alistair's gold tooth glinted in the candlelight. "Well, ma'am," he said slowly as if choosing his words carefully, "I don't reckon I'm a real earl. Not proper-like on paper 'n such. But according to my mum, I can trace my heritage back to the gentry."

Rosaleen smiled at the wink Alistair shot in her direction. But her smile quickly faded when she turned it toward Jacob. The frown lines dragging down his mouth held no trace of the young minister's usual good humor.

She had no doubt it was Alistair's presence that had soured Jacob's mood. Did Jacob simply find the gambler unsavory? Or was he brooding over the kiss he'd seen Alistair give her that morning? She couldn't help hoping it was the latter.

૨ઠ

The scowling face staring back at Jacob from the bureau mirror seemed foreign. He didn't like the way he looked these days, and he certainly didn't like the way he felt. He wiped off the remnants of the shaving soap with a quick swipe of the towel and then threw it hard onto the washstand.

Buttoning his dress shirt, he gazed out his upstairs window at Mulberry Street below. Madison was just beginning to stir to life this Fourth of July. Though the morning sun slanting through his window promised a beautiful Independence Day, worry over Rosaleen had robbed his heart of all celebratory feelings.

He'd been glad to notice that the gambler, Alistair Ralston, spent most of his time away from the boardinghouse. Gambling and running his ruses down in one or another of the taverns along the riverfront, Jacob guessed.

He didn't like the familiar way the man acted around Rosaleen. To be honest, he didn't like the familiarity Rosaleen showed Ralston, either.

The prayer he'd been praying in the week since Ralston's

appearance rose again from his heart. *Oh God, please guide her. Just guide her.*

His fingers moved automatically as he tied his black silk cravat. Sighing, he licked his lips, remembering the one sweet kiss he and Rosaleen had shared. Recalling how she'd clung to him—her eager response to his kiss—he couldn't believe she didn't care for him.

When Sophie Schuler appeared unexpectedly in Madison, he'd steeled his resolve to renew a relationship with the girl he'd courted two years ago. With all good intentions, he'd tried to ignore his feelings for Rosaleen and lash his errant heart to the hitching post of practicality.

The touch of Rosaleen's lips against his had shattered that resolve. To encourage Sophie when his heart was bound to Rosaleen would be dishonest and potentially hurtful.

Thankfully, Sophie Schuler had become one of Madison's social butterflies and showed little interest in renewing their relationship. The previous Sunday, she'd casually mentioned that she'd be celebrating the holiday by joining a group of Madison's youthful elite on a railroad excursion to Columbus.

Ironically, it wasn't Sophie who seemed to be impeding the deeper relationship Jacob would like to grow between himself and Rosaleen, but Rosaleen herself. He felt heat spread from his neck to his scalp remembering her troubling reaction to his kiss. He still stung from the way she'd fled the church, as if he might do her harm.

She was, after all, a new widow. A decent amount of time needed to pass before he could, in all decorum, attempt to court her. Yet he'd seen no sign of decorum on her part when he watched her happily kiss Alistair Ralston.

And then there was the fact that she'd not yet given her heart to Christ. However, hope had been growing in Jacob that she might be nearing a decision about that. Sunday after Sunday, he watched her lovely eyes glisten with tears while she listened with what seemed rapt attention as he preached of Christ's love and salvation. He'd even noticed her following along in the Bible he'd given her.

Jacob shrugged on his dress coat, glad that he and Rosaleen would be spending most of the day with Becky, Ephraim, and their children. He silently blessed his sister for inviting Rosaleen to the Independence Day picnic at their home. Besides affording him an opportunity to make amends for his rash behavior at the church last week, it gave Rosaleen a reason to not spend time with Alistair Ralston.

As he entered the parlor, his heart did its usual little flip-flop when his gaze found Rosaleen. Looking stunning in the green sprigged muslin dress Becky had given her, she sat on the sofa beside Alistair Ralston. Her lighthearted laughter, directed at the gambler, sent a surge of jealousy through Jacob.

"No, Alistair, I know better than to play that shell game with you. And I certainly wouldn't bet my brooch." Her hand went to the ever-present brooch at the center of her bodice. When her gaze drifted to the doorway, she popped up from the sofa, the laugh dying on her lips. "Oh, Jacob," she said breathlessly, her demeanor resembling that of a guilty child.

"Are you ready, Rosaleen?" The forced smile hurt Jacob's face.

"The offer stands, Rosaleen." Alistair gave her a wink that ignited a flame of anger in Jacob.

Rosaleen accepted Jacob's proffered arm. "Then I should expect it will grow tired standing," she shot back at Alistair with a nervous-sounding giggle.

As they walked up Mulberry Street toward Main-Cross, Jacob fought to keep his voice light. Surely the man had not offered Rosaleen marriage. "What was Mr. Ralston's offer, if I might be so bold as to ask?"

"Oh, my brooch," she said with a light laugh. "Alistair knows good and well I'll not part with it, yet he can't seem to help himself from trying."

"Just how well do you know Mr. Ralston?"

"It seems I've known him forever. Like me, he's been moving from riverboat to riverboat most of his life. I think of him almost as an older brother."

"Do you miss it—life on the riverboats?" Jacob needed to learn the answers to the concerns pressing against his heart. In Ralston's vernacular, he might as well "go for broke."

"No."

He felt immense relief at the definitive tone of her voice. "You don't plan on going back to it then?"

She gave a little shake of her head. "No, not to the riverboats."

"But you do plan on leaving Madison. . . ." Jacob sent up a quick prayer that she would dispel his suspicions. It went unanswered.

"Yes," she murmured, sending his heart plummeting and confirming what he realized he'd known all along but had not allowed himself to admit.

"Where do you plan to go? You said you had no other family." *Maybe if she has nowhere else to go, I can convince her—*

"New York. When I was at Mrs. Griswold's Academy, a concert pianist, Maestro Levitsky, visited the academy and heard me play. He told me I had great talent, and if I could get to New York, he would help me become a concert pianist." Her voice deflated. "Donovan had promised to take me, but now. . ."

Learning of her plans to travel to New York jarred Jacob. Hope of her staying in Madison shriveled. He had no right to ask her to abandon her dream.

He forced his lips into a smile. "You'd be the toast of the New York concert halls."

They walked the next two blocks in silence until he realized he'd never apologized for frightening her at the church. He decided this might be as good a time as any. Perhaps then, the stiff formality that had grown between them would relax a bit.

"Rosaleen, I—I wanted to let you know, I'm sorry about what happened last week. . .in the church." His conscience chafed against the lie. He indeed regretted having frightened her, but he could not make his heart sorry for the kiss.

"It's all right, Jacob. I've thought no more of it, and neither should you."

Her quiet words were like a dagger through his heart, but he noticed her gaze remained fixed on the gravel beneath their feet.

At last, they reached the church on Main-Cross Street where the children of Madison's Sunday schools had gathered for a parade. The boys held patriotic-colored banners while the girls trailed red, white, and blue ribbons.

Grinning, Jacob returned Daniel's sharp salute. But he found little joy in the procession or the day's celebrations. Rosaleen's plans to leave Madison weighted his heart like a stone. How long did he have to win her heart to Christ—and to him?

Later, they followed the procession down to Ohio Street on the riverfront where local dignitaries gave addresses. But Jacob barely noticed the different speakers and their talk of imminent war with Mexico. With Rosaleen beside him, filling his senses, all other stimuli faded.

Following the addresses, the gunnery sergeant of the militia presided over a cannon salute. A burst of laughter and cheers trailed the gun's loud report. When Rosaleen jumped back at the boom, Jacob caught her around the waist, saving her from tumbling backward into the crowd behind them. Giggling, they clung to one another for one sweet, beautiful moment amid the acrid smell of gunpowder floating over the crowd.

Oh God, if I could only hold her like this forever. If I could only convince her never to leave Madison.

"Tell 'em to fire the cannon again, Papa." Daniel's innocent appeal to Ephraim shattered the spell, and they dissolved into laughter.

At the conclusion of the town's festivities, Jacob and Rosaleen joined his sister and her family at their home on Main-Cross Street. There, Rosaleen, Jacob, and Ephraim settled themselves on quilts spread beneath a large maple tree in the front yard, while Becky slipped into the house to feed baby Lucy.

Young Daniel marched up to Jacob and Rosaleen, offering glasses of lemonade.

"Thank you, Daniel." Jacob grinned at his nephew's hands, wet with the sticky beverage sloshing over the glasses' rims.

"Better than the Fourth of July refreshment you tried ten years ago, wouldn't you say, Jacob?" Ephraim asked with a sly, mischievous grin.

Jacob took a sip of the sweetened, tart drink and groaned at his brother-in-law's teasing reference to his one and only sampling of home brew at the age of sixteen.

"What Fourth of July refreshment?" Rosaleen perked, turning an interested smile toward him.

"When I was sixteen, I stupidly took a dare to drink half a keg of home brew." Forced to recount the embarrassing episode to Rosaleen, Jacob shot Ephraim a glare that set his brother-in-law to chuckling.

"You? But you're a preacher." She blinked, and then her eyes widened to puzzled, blue-green pools.

Her obvious bewilderment concerned more than amused Jacob. "I wasn't then and hadn't yet given my heart and life to Christ."

"But I thought preachers were—I mean, never did. . ." A rosy blush prettily stained the confused look on her face.

"You thought preachers were perfect?" Jacob couldn't help smiling as he rushed to her rescue, but the depth of her misunderstanding troubled him. What other misconceptions might she have about preachers or Christians in general? "Romans 3:23 says, 'For all have sinned, and come short of the glory of God.' No one is perfect; only Christ is. We are all saved by His grace, Rosaleen."

"You really believe that?"

Astounded, Jacob met her skeptical look. "Of course. The apostle Paul tells us in chapter one, verse sixteen of his letter to the Romans, 'For I am not ashamed of the gospel of Christ:

for it is the power of God unto salvation to every one that believeth.'"

Becky poked her head out the front door. "Lucy's asleep, so Rosaleen, if you'll help me in the kitchen, we'll have the fried chicken, potato salad, and apple pie out here in two shakes."

His heart in conflict, Jacob watched Rosaleen follow his sister into the house. He prayed that their previous exchange indicated Rosaleen might be considering giving her heart to Christ. If not, how could he love a nonbeliever? Yet he could more easily empty the Ohio River than stop loving Rosaleen Archer.

After lunch, they gathered in the parlor where Rosaleen entertained them at the piano with renditions of patriotic songs. They all sang along to the stirring "Ode to George Washington" and "The Grand Constitution." Daniel especially enjoyed "Yankee Doodle," marching around the parlor as he sang.

When Rosaleen played a popular tune called "The Girl I Left Behind Me," its haunting melody permeated Jacob's heart like a melancholy fog. He had to wonder if it might be *he* who'd be left behind, knowing she planned to leave for New York as soon as possible. He found it even more worrisome to think that she might not be leaving alone. He felt his brows slide together in a frown as the image of Alistair Ralston muscled into his thoughts.

eleven

One evening several days after the Fourth of July celebrations, Rosaleen sat on her little straw tick in her attic room. Rubbing her eyes in the sputtering light of the tallow candle, she read the words from Romans 1:16 that Jacob had quoted. "For I am not ashamed of the gospel of Christ: for it is the power of God unto salvation to every one that believeth."

Every one that believeth.

Rosaleen wanted to believe it meant her. She wanted to believe it more than she'd ever wanted to believe anything.

"For it is the power of God unto salvation to every one that believeth." Her whispered breath caressed each word. Perhaps there was hope. Perhaps the promise in that scripture *did* include her.

A quiet rap at her door yanked her attention from the scriptures, and she dropped the Bible to her mattress. "Yes, who is it?"

When no one answered, her heart began to pound. She crossed the little room, her bare feet padding softly on the floorboards.

"Who is it?" She managed the three breathless words, her face pressed against the door and her heart beating like a kettledrum in her chest.

"It's Andrew. Open the door."

At the rasped whisper, relief drained the strength from her limbs. With unsteady fingers, she unlocked the door. What on earth could Andrew want?

Panic gripped Rosaleen. *Patsey.* Was Patsey ill? Was the baby coming too early? If so, why hadn't Andrew simply gone to fetch Dr. Morgan?

When she opened the door, bewilderment replaced fear.

A young black woman and two small children dressed in near rags stood trembling beside Andrew.

Suddenly Rosaleen remembered a conversation she had last week with Patsey. When Patsey asked her if she would be willing to hide runaway slaves, Rosaleen had agreed to help. Patsey went on to explain that Mrs. Buchanan had used the attic room from time to time to hide runaways when other accommodations could not be found. Although eager to help slaves on their road to freedom, Rosaleen hadn't expected such an opportunity to occur so soon.

"They jis crossed the Jordan and need a place to stay. Maybe a day. Maybe two," Andrew told her in a whispered rasp. He darted anxious glances down the stairway then ushered the three into Rosaleen's room and pulled the door behind them. "Mrs. Buchanan knows. Cain't tell Rev'rend. If asked, he'd be obliged not to lie. Cain't risk it. Can you act like nothin's different? Nothin' at all?"

Still a bit stunned, Rosaleen nodded. These were passengers on the Underground Railroad. She surmised the "Jordan" referred to the Ohio River.

"This is Sally, Lizzie, and Elijah," Andrew informed her.

Rosaleen's heart went out to the frail woman and the little boy and girl. Both children, who looked about Daniel Morgan's age, seemed to struggle just to keep their eyes open.

"But there's only one mattress." Rosaleen's mind raced. How would they all manage, even for a couple of days? The little attic room was barely large enough for one.

"They don't need no mattress. This floor's better'n what they're used to. Don't tell nobody. Not even Patsey. She don't know. Jis go on like nothin's different. Don't let on. Their lives depend on it." With those whispered instructions, Andrew left, quietly closing the door behind him.

Rosaleen hurried to lock the door, then without saying a word, guided the two children to the mattress and covered them with the quilt. The poor, exhausted little things fell asleep the moment their heads touched the mattress.

As she lay down beside Sally on the hard floorboards, Rosaleen shifted from side to side, unable to find a comfortable position. Yet the unexpected situation had left her heart and mind in far more unease than her body.

She'd been reading the words of Jesus, trying to learn how she could most please God. If scant chance existed that she might find salvation, she felt it depended upon being careful not to displease Him.

Jacob had said, "All have sinned," yet her guardian had called her irredeemable. Her only hope, she reasoned, was to be perfect from now on. That chance, she realized with dismay, might just have been snatched from her. The memory of Wilfred Maguire's voice booming from his pulpit in Natchez sank her hope.

" 'All liars, shall have their part in the lake which burneth with fire and brimstone.'"

Opal knew about the presence of the runaways, and whatever suspicions Patsey might have, Rosaleen knew she'd never ask. Jacob, however, seemed to have been watching her comings and goings more closely since Alistair's arrival. Now, she might very well be forced to lie to Jacob in order to protect him as well as the runaways.

❧

For the next two days, with Mrs. Buchanan's help, Rosaleen managed to keep her three "guests" supplied with food and fresh water. The tiny attic space was stifling in the July heat, yet she dare not open the little casement window even a crack.

None of the three runaways had spoken a word to her during the time they'd been cloistered in her room.

Rosaleen made sure no one was around as she headed up the stairs to the attic carrying a pitcher of fresh water and a towel-draped washbowl filled with bread and ham. Setting the pitcher down, she slowly opened the door and poked her head into the room.

Sally's and her children's eyes grew large with looks of fear, followed quickly by ones of stark relief. Yet all remained mute, grateful smiles stretching their sweat-drenched faces.

Retrieving the pitcher and bowl, Rosaleen choked back tears. She wished she could offer them assurances of safety as well as sustenance, but all she could do was pour them fresh cups of well water and offer them the food.

Later, as she walked into Jacob's vacant room to gather the bed linens for the weekly laundry, the fugitive mother and children clung to her mind. She found it amazing that anyone, especially children, could remain so silent for such a long time.

She found even more astounding the fact that Patsey seemed entirely oblivious to Sally's, Lizzie's, and Elijah's presence. Andrew had said she didn't know, and her demeanor bore out his claim. Though Rosaleen understood Andrew's intention to protect Patsey as well as the runaways, she couldn't imagine not disclosing such knowledge to a mate.

Rosaleen recalled happy talks she'd shared with Donovan. How they'd laughed over silly things like a lady's outrageous hat or an unusual landmark along the river.

She brushed a tear from her cheek, spread a fresh sheet over Jacob's bed, and tucked the ends under the feather mattress. When she gazed about the neat little room, her heart ached. His well-worn Bible on the bureau, his razor lying on the washstand, and the blue and white striped calico work shirt hanging from the bedpost all reminded her of the man who owned her heart.

She lifted the shirt from the bedpost to add it to the bundle of laundry. Closing her eyes, she laid it against her cheek, inhaling his familiar scent. Once again, she could feel his lips, soft and tender, caressing hers.

Visions of what life might be like as Jacob's wife played before her mind's eye. She imagined herself giggling in his arms as they shared humorous anecdotes. She could see his blue eyes laughing into hers and her reaching a finger up to trace the thin scar that ran the length of his cheek. His eyes would close, his mouth seeking hers. She could almost taste the sweetness of his kisses and feel the comfort of his arms.

More tears slipped down her face. She had no hope of such dreams ever coming true. No right to even dream. That future did not belong to her. It belonged to Sophie Schuler.

The best she could hope for would be to keep Jacob's respect. Now that, too, had been put in jeopardy. So far, she'd managed to avoid lying to him. But Elijah had developed a cough, causing the boy to press his little face into a pillow to muffle the sound. Sooner or later, Rosaleen feared she'd need to fabricate a story to explain the sounds.

She gathered the pile of linens in her arms and started down the stairs.

"Whoa there!"

At the bottom of the stairs, Rosaleen gasped. She'd walked straight into Alistair Ralston.

"Hey, come with me down to the Billiard Saloon tonight. We'll have some fun fleecing salesmen and farmers." He wrapped his long arms around her, sheets and all.

"I have work to do, and then I have to get up early in the morning, Alistair." She wriggled out of his grasp and attempted to walk around him.

He caught her around the waist, his muscular arm clamping her hard against him. Until now, she'd never felt afraid of Alistair. His friendly smile and chuckle did not match the roguish glint in his eyes. "You could send me signals like you used to do for your dad. With your looks and my skill, we could clean up, Rosaleen. You know we could."

"That's not my life anymore, Alistair. That's not who I am now." During her time here in Madison she'd begun to feel decent, and she liked that feeling. She wouldn't let Alistair—or anyone for that matter—suck her back into the unscrupulous gambling life. Besides, at the moment she had Sally, Lizzie, and Elijah to see to.

"Think on it, love." With a wicked wink, he pressed a quick kiss on her cheek. "You can find me at the Billiard."

As Alistair strode out the front door, her head pivoted

toward a sound near the parlor doorway. Her face grew hot at Jacob's incredulous gaze. How much had he heard?

Her heart deflated when he said nothing. He simply turned and walked back into the parlor.

Rosaleen wanted to march into the parlor and tell Jacob she had no intention of joining Alistair at the Billiard Saloon. It took all her willpower to walk past the parlor and toward the backyard washtub. A conversation with Jacob would simply be too dangerous.

twelve

Jacob snapped the Bible shut and pushed away from his desk. Heaving a deep sigh, he rubbed his hand over his face. He'd searched the Proverbs for God's wisdom yet found no answers to the troubles plaguing his heart.

Rosaleen was driving him crazy.

After giving her the Bible, he'd hoped she might begin asking questions about the scriptures. He'd been encouraged by the glimmer of interest she showed at Becky's Fourth of July picnic.

Lately, however, she'd shown little interest in speaking with him about the scriptures, or any other subject for that matter. Clenching his jaw, Jacob glanced toward the parlor doorway. He felt sure he knew who had caused the change in her.

Alistair Ralston.

Three nights ago, he'd heard the muffled but unmistakable sound of a man's boots on the stairway leading to her attic room. He and Alistair Ralston were the only two men presently living in the boardinghouse. Jacob hated the images forming in his mind but could find no logic to explain them away.

Only an hour ago, he'd caught her, once again, in Ralston's arms. What was worse, the man had kissed her and invited her to the infamous Billiard Saloon.

Jacob gave the chair a resolute shove against the desk. It was useless to try to work on his sermon with his mind insisting on steering toward dark thoughts. He might as well go work on the church. At least there, he could see the results of an hour's endeavors.

At the intersection of Mulberry and Main-Cross, he was surprised to see Rosaleen leaving Maynard's Apothecary.

A sudden fear seized him. Perhaps she'd been feeling unwell. That could explain her reticent mood of late.

"Rosaleen, are you all right?" He glanced at the basket on her arm.

"Oh, yes." Her face flushed a deep pink, and she scooted an amber bottle beneath a green and white gingham cloth. "Just—just an errand." Her face looked as if it might crack with the force of her smile.

"Are you sure, because if you're unwell. . ."

"No. I'm quite all right. Quite." She looked down Mulberry as if eager to be away and transferred the basket to her arm farthest from him.

What was she hiding? He wished he'd gotten a better look at that bottle. He'd thought it looked suspiciously like a whiskey bottle the instant before she'd hidden it. Maynard's sold spirits as well as medicines. Could it be for Ralston? But then, wouldn't the man simply get his liquor at the Billiard Saloon?

"I was just on my way to the church but would be glad to carry your basket and accompany you back to the boardinghouse first." Perhaps God had given him this opportunity to speak with her.

"No, thank you just the same, but I wouldn't want to detain you from your work on the church." Her rushed answer tumbled out while her glance darted about as if looking for escape.

"I don't mind, really. . . ," Jacob began.

"Reverend Hale. Ma'am." Constable Rafe Arbuckle's voice intruded as he stepped toward them dragging his hat off his shock of salt-and-pepper hair. "The sheriff got wind of a bunch of runaway slaves. Just wonderin' if you'd seen any different faces, you bein' situated near Georgetown an' all."

Jacob stiffened. "No. No, I haven't." He knew the sheriff was a hot pro-slavery man. In the two years he'd been in Madison, Jacob would have liked to help the Chapmans and Opal in their work with the Underground Railroad. However, being a minister, he knew he'd be questioned often. He'd learned from Orville that he could best help the organization by being oblivious to its movements.

"I—I need to get back to the boardinghouse and help with the washing," Rosaleen murmured. Before he could stop her, she hurried down Mulberry Street.

"Don't mean to be a bother. Just supposed to ask, that's all," Rafe said, his voice apologetic as he shifted from foot to foot.

Jacob's heart sank at his lost opportunity to talk with Rosaleen. He dragged his gaze from her fleeting figure back to Rafe. He couldn't help feeling sympathy for the constable. Rafe Arbuckle was a good man who'd been sent on a distasteful errand. He gave Arbuckle an understanding smile and clapped his hand on the man's shoulder. "That's all right, Rafe. You're just doing your duty."

As he walked to the church, Jacob realized that instead of learning any answers to his questions about Rosaleen, he'd been presented with even more questions.

"Be ye not unequally yoked together with unbelievers."

The words from Second Corinthians screamed through his mind. But he *was* yoked. His heart was inextricably bound to hers.

The sight of the new church building no longer brought him the joy it once had. Each soul won to Christ in this building would be precious. Yet if he failed with Rosaleen, he feared he'd be forever haunted by the one soul his heart most longed to claim for Christ.

Oh God, help me to win her for You, or disentangle my heart from hers and emancipate me from this misery.

❧

Rosaleen jerked up from her bedroom floor with a start. She'd slept in her day dress expecting the knock, yet the soft rap set her heart pounding.

"Rosaleen." Andrew Chapman's voice slowed her heart to a canter.

Without a word, she unlocked the door and let him in.

"Train's a'comin'."

"Already?"

Andrew nodded.

The encounter this afternoon with constable Arbuckle had been unnerving. She remembered how her heart had pounded and her knees had gone weak, fearing she would be directly questioned about the runaway slaves.

She knew the sooner they could move on, the better for all involved. Yet in the last two days, she'd become accustomed to the presence of Sally and the children. The sadness she felt at the thought of parting with them surprised her.

Sniffing back tears, she gently woke Lizzie and Elijah. It tugged at her heart to see the way they accepted the intrusion. She, too, had known what it was to be treated as less than human. Like these slaves, she'd lived with terror, accepting it as a matter of course. The cruelty she'd experienced in her own life caused her heart to bond with these innocent unfortunates who simply longed to breathe free. With tears streaming down her face, Rosaleen hugged the little ones in turn.

"God bless you, Miss Rosaleen."

Stunned at the first words Sally had uttered to her, Rosaleen hugged the frail woman. She pressed into Sally's hands the bottle of tonic that had done wonders for Elijah's cough. "Just stay well. All of you."

"Need you to come, too."

Startled, Rosaleen raised her face to Andrew's. "Why?"

Whispering, he kept his words pared to the essentials. "'Case we're stopped an' somebody asks questions. Patsey ain't been feelin' none too good. Jis fetchin' you to see about Patsey, that's all."

A still, small voice spoke to Rosaleen's heart, nudging her to the straw mattress. She'd been reading the words of Jesus. With each new day, the longing in her heart grew stronger to obey His words. This evening she'd been reading from the nineteenth chapter of Matthew. Hungering for Christ's acceptance, she'd fixed her attention on Jesus' response to a young man who'd asked how he might attain eternal life. She'd read verse twenty-one over and over until she'd committed it to memory.

"Jesus said unto him, If thou wilt be perfect, go and sell that thou hast, and give to the poor, and thou shalt have treasure in heaven: and come and follow me."

Without hesitation or regret, she reached into the mattress slit and grasped the little calico bag then turned to Andrew. "I want them to have this. It's only six dollars, but maybe it will help."

"Bless you, Miss Rosaleen." The look of gratitude on Andrew's face as he tucked the bag inside his shirt was all the reward she needed.

Praying had now become a habit with Rosaleen. Though she remained unsure if Jesus actually heard the prayers, they simply made her feel better. She prayed hard as their little ragamuffin band stole down the stairs and out to Andrew's waiting wagon.

In the darkness, Rosaleen could just make out the farm wagon piled high with straw. While she wondered if Sally and the children would have to burrow deep inside, she watched Andrew reach beneath the wagon bed and unlatch a little door. To her amazement, the three runaways crawled up into the false wagon bottom, and Andrew fastened the door behind them.

Her heart hammering, Rosaleen bounced on the buckboard seat beside Andrew. They wended their way through the moonless night, northeast out of Madison. Andrew had told her the next station was at a place he'd called Eagle Hollow. He said the distance would be about ten miles, but the crooked, elevated path made it seem twice as long.

At last, they stopped at a little stone house, and Andrew rapped softly at the door.

The door creaked open, revealing no light within the home's dark interior.

"I have the cargo you ordered." Andrew's whispered words carried through the still night air to the wagon.

No one answered, but a moment later he was at the back of the wagon helping the three runaways from their cramped hiding place.

Rosaleen's eyes strained in the darkness to catch one last glimpse of the three who'd shared her attic room for the past two days and three nights. A prayer rent from her anxious heart. *Jesus, be with them. You healed the sick, raised the dead, and stilled the tempest. Please, please just keep them safe.*

"Will they make it?" Rosaleen couldn't help asking the question as she and Andrew jostled over the rut-pocked road toward Madison.

"Good chance. Conductors from here on are pretty reliable."

"Is Patsey really sick?" Sudden concern for her friend tightened Rosaleen's voice. She hated the thought of Patsey sick at home alone without her husband beside her.

"She'll be all right." His teeth flashed a smile in the darkness. "Jis took a hankerin' for some fried mush then couldn't abide the grease. She be sleepin' now." Rosaleen heard love and longing in his soft voice. "I can walk back to the boardinghouse from here," she said as they neared the Georgetown area of Madison.

Andrew shook his head. "Ain't fittin'. . .or safe. Like I said, Patsey be sleepin'. 'Nother few minutes won't make no difference to her."

Only moments after Andrew dropped Rosaleen off near the boardinghouse and headed back to Georgetown, she understood his concerns about her walking home. Her heart jumped to her throat when she saw a large shadowy figure looming in the dark street ahead less than a half block from where she stood. As the figure neared, weaving its way toward her from the south, she heaved a sigh of relief. It was only Alistair, making his way back to the boardinghouse from a night of gambling down at the Billiard Saloon on Ohio Street's riverfront. A good deal worse for the wear, it would seem.

"Rose'leen, m'little Rose'leen," Alistair slurred as he grasped her around the waist. "Too late, too late," he lamented, wagging an unsteady finger in her face. "Gamblin' done, drinkin' done. Time to go t'bed."

He stumbled and nearly fell when she pushed away from his whiskey-soaked breath. "I'd say *bed* is exactly where you belong, Alistair." She turned her face south toward the fresh breezes blowing off the river.

Wrapping her arm as far around him as it would go, Rosaleen prayed she'd be able to maneuver Alistair up to his room on the second floor without waking Jacob or Opal. She cringed at his every hiccup, laugh, and slurred verse of "Old Dan Tucker" until they reached the door of his room.

When she pushed open the door, he stumbled in, carrying her with him. Alistair fell back onto the bed with a crash, and she found herself pulled on top of him, his arms clamped around her. Pushing hard against his chest, she extricated herself from his grasp, but fell backward, landing on the floor with a *boom*. She could hear him snoring, already dead to the world.

Gasping for breath, she struggled to her feet. Her hair pulled loose from its pins and tumbled to her shoulders. It was in this disheveled state that she met Jacob's shocked gaze as she exited Alistair's room.

The lit candle in his hand illuminated his stunned features. He stood in his nightshirt, his blond head poking out from his bedroom door. "Everything all right?" he asked in a frosty voice.

"Yes—yes." Mortified, Rosaleen pushed the straggling hair from her face, realizing how stupid and ineffectual the motion must look. Racing past him, she hurried to the end of the hall and the stairway that lead to her attic room. Behind her, the sound of his door snapping shut felt like a lance through her heart.

thirteen

Rosaleen fidgeted on her seat beside the piano. For the first time since she'd begun playing for Sunday services, she felt eager for the benediction.

She hadn't been able to look Jacob in the eye after her humiliating encounter with him outside Alistair's room. His demeanor toward her had not thawed one degree, and her heart screamed to give him a true accounting of last night's events. But even if she could tell him about her involvement in helping the runaway slaves, would he believe her if she tried to explain?

This morning, his sermon, taken from the second chapter of Proverbs, dealt with wisdom. She wondered if he'd chosen the theme especially for her benefit, though his gaze seemed to diligently avoid hers.

" 'To deliver thee from the strange woman, even from the stranger which flattereth with her words,' " Jacob read from verse sixteen.

She remembered the look on Jacob's face when he'd watched her stumble from Alistair's room. What emotions had she seen playing across his features in the vacillating light and shadows of the flickering candle? Astonishment? Of course. Anger? Disgust? Had he, like Wilfred Maguire, decided that she was beyond redemption?

The next passage of scripture that boomed from Jacob's voice seemed directed at her. " 'But the wicked shall be cut off from the earth, and the transgressors shall be rooted out of it.' "

Wicked.

There it was again—the word Reverend Maguire had consistently attached to her. And now she'd heard it from Jacob's own mouth. It reverberated through her stricken heart as if the very ax of the Almighty had fallen, severing her from any prospect of salvation. The hope she'd nurtured during hours of searching the Gospels for Christ's acceptance had all at once been consumed to ashes and blown away. Reverend Maguire had been right. She was wicked—wicked and irredeemable.

Struggling for breath, Rosaleen knew she had to get away. Gathering her skirts in her fists, she leaped from her seat and ran from the room, through the boardinghouse, and out the kitchen door. Her vision obscured by tears, she ran on trembling legs as if to escape the wrath of God. She hadn't even realized how far she'd gone until several minutes after she sank to the bench beside Jacob's new church.

Lifting her head, she gazed two blocks south where the sunlight danced over the Ohio River like silver sprites. A strong southwest breeze carried the dank, fishy scent of the river that blended with the fresh smell of new lumber. Cool river breezes dried her tears and brushed the leaves of Orville Whitaker's willow tree against her shoulder.

She'd so wanted to believe the promises of Christ were meant for her. But after the things Bill McGurty had forced her to do, how could she expect Jesus to look upon her with anything but disgust?

"Blessed are the pure in heart: for they shall see God." Jesus' words from the fifth chapter of Matthew seemed to seal her doom. Convinced she'd been sullied beyond repair, she pressed her face in her hands and sobbed.

꙳

Frantic to learn what had caused Rosaleen to flee the parlor, Jacob brought the sermon to an abrupt close. After offering a quick benediction, he began searching the house.

He raced from room to room. Panic rose inside him when he failed to find her. If she'd felt sick, surely she would have gone to her room. Yet he found the little attic room unoccupied. He forced himself to knock at Ralston's door. Receiving no answer, he opened it and found it vacant as well.

He shoved his fingers through his hair in an attempt to calm his mind. Surely she hadn't gone off with the man.

Think, Jacob, think! Oh God, You know where she is. Please show me.

The second the idea entered his mind, he flew down the stairs, out the kitchen door, and across town.

His heart fluctuated between relief and concern when he found her crying beneath Orville's willow. Her agonized sobs ripped at his heart. Was she ashamed of what she'd done last night? Had the man forced her against her will? Or had last night not been the first time?

He remembered what he'd heard two nights ago. Footsteps and whispers in the wee hours of the morning on the floor above his. He'd heard the sound of a man's boots on the stairs leading up to Rosaleen's room. When these facts assembled themselves in Jacob's mind, the picture they painted sickened him. Yet what other conclusion could there be?

Oh God, help me to show her love, not condemnation.

"Rosaleen"—he knelt at her feet and tenderly took her hands into his—"please tell me what has distressed you so. Is it Mr. Ralston and what happened between the two of you last night?"

"No!" She raised her face to his, a combination of anger, pain, and frustration brimming in her eyes. "Nothing happened between Alistair and me last night. Nothing!" Pulling her hands from his, she balled her fists in her lap. "He was drunk. I was just helping him back to his room. If you don't want to believe me. . ." She turned her tear-streaked face toward the river.

"I believe you, Rosaleen." Even as he said the words, there was a part of him that still wondered. "Then what is wrong?"

She swung her hurt-filled face back to his. "I wanted to belong. I've been reading the Gospels. I thought maybe Jesus would accept me, but I was only fooling myself." Her voice broke over another sob. "Your sermon today—I'm the strange woman you need to be delivered from. I'm part of the wicked that shall be cut off from the earth."

Jacob groaned. It pained him to think that his own sermon had contributed to her agony. "When the scriptures speak of the 'wicked,' they are referring to those who turn away from the Lord. You just said you've been searching for Jesus' acceptance." His voice softened with his melting heart. "My dear Rosaleen, He's already accepted you."

"I'm not sure that's possible."

"Why on earth would you think such a thing?" Had nothing he'd tried to teach her taken root?

"Because I'm dirty. Dirty, wicked, and irredeemable. You don't really know who I am. You don't know all that's happened to me."

"What, Rosaleen? What happened that makes you think Jesus wouldn't accept you?" Jacob attempted to put his arms around her, to comfort her, but she pulled away. His heart ached to bring her peace. "Jesus loves you, Rosaleen, and there is no sin too great for Him to forgive."

"You don't know! You don't know what's happened to me. . .or what I've done. Donovan didn't die the night of the accident," she blurted, gasping between sobs. "Black Jack Bill McGurty, a gambler and murderer, shot him. Then he took me, and for six months. . .for six months. . ." She couldn't seem to bring herself to finish the sentence. "An hour before the boiler exploded on the *Cortland Belle*, I'd considered taking my own life." Her body shook with her crying.

Stunned by the revelations, Jacob could only wonder what other dark facts she might have kept from him. Yet his heart broke at her anguish. This time she allowed him to gather her into his arms, hold her, caress her. Now he understood her night terrors. The unspeakable horrors she must have endured. He rocked her in his arms, pressing his lips against her hair. A feeling of protectiveness flooded Jacob. He knew without a doubt, for the rest of his life, he wanted to love this woman and make her feel safe.

Oh God, just help me make her feel safe.

"It's all right, my sweet," he murmured. "I won't let anyone hurt you ever again. Jesus loves you, and I love you. I love you, Rosaleen."

"Don't say that! You're wrong!" Tears streamed down her face. She jumped up from the bench and stepped away as if fearing her nearness might contaminate him. "Didn't you hear me? I was born wicked and shall always be wicked. I'm irredeemable!"

"Rosaleen, no one is irredeemable. Where did you ever get such an idea?" Frustration set a sharp edge to Jacob's rising voice.

"The Reverend Wilfred Maguire, my former guardian. He is the minister of a church three times the size of yours." It hurt when she cast a look of disdain toward the new church of which he felt so proud.

"He's wrong, Rosaleen." Furious at the man for what he'd told her, Jacob couldn't keep the anger from his voice. "Why would a minister, of all people, say such a thing?"

She drew a deep, ragged breath. "He said he'd seen women like me and my mother all his life. He said we were just like the loose, common women who'd lured his father away from his mother and broke her heart. When I refused to denounce my mother as a harlot, he declared me wicked and irredeemable. He quoted scripture that says something about God not having mercy upon me because I was conceived in shame." She looked at him with sad, vacant eyes. "God hates me."

Jacob groaned. How could a minister of the gospel, because of a hurt from his past, so grotesquely twist the scriptures?

"Of course God doesn't hate you. That is just ridiculous! I believe the scripture you cited is from the book of Hosea and refers to the children of Israel who had strayed from God." He took a deep breath. She did not need his reproach. It was not her fault that she'd been told such a cruel thing. Guiding her back to the bench, he sat down beside her and folded her hands in his.

Oh God, give me the right words that will bring her peace and lead her at last to You.

"Rosaleen, God loves all souls, no matter how they came into this world. Psalm 139 talks about how God knows us and loves us even before we are born. 'For thou hast possessed my reins: thou hast covered me in my mother's womb.'"

He searched the blue-green depths of her eyes glistening with tears. "Have you read any in the Gospel of John?"

She shook her head. "No."

"John 3:16–17, says, 'For God so loved the world, that he gave his only begotten Son, that whosoever believeth in him should not perish, but have everlasting life. For God sent not his Son into the world to condemn the world; but that the world through him might be saved.' The *world*, Rosaleen. You are part of the world. Christ doesn't reject anyone. People reject *Him*. You can be lost only by rejecting Christ."

"But Jesus talks about being pure. 'Blessed are the pure in heart: for they shall see God.'"

Jacob couldn't help grinning in spite of himself. "You *have* been reading the Gospels."

"I'm not pure, Jacob." She closed her eyes.

Watching tears slide from beneath her lashes to streak down her face rent Jacob's heart. He could only imagine the terror-filled scenes playing behind her closed eyelids. "Rosaleen, what happened to you was not your fault, not your sin. Remember what I told you on the Fourth of July? 'For all have sinned, and come short of the glory of God.' The prophet Isaiah, speaking of Christ, said, 'Though your sins be as scarlet, they shall be as white as snow; though they be red like crimson, they shall be as wool.' There is no sin too great for Christ to forgive. He paid the price for everyone's sins and left them on the cross. All that is required of you is to accept His gift of salvation. Do you believe that?"

"I—I want to."

Jacob felt a flash of frustration at her hesitation. How much plainer could he make it? She either wanted to accept Christ or she didn't. Perhaps she wasn't as eager as she pretended to leave behind the sinful life.

Even if nothing had happened between her and Ralston last night, she'd come in with him so had obviously been out with him. Jacob had heard Ralston invite her to the Billiard Saloon. That, coupled with the suspicious sounds he'd heard coming from the third floor several nights ago, caused him to question her sincerity and lash out at her.

"Do you?" His dry tone reflected his doubts as the old insecurities crept back into his heart. Was he so unpersuasive a preacher he couldn't even bring the woman he loved to the Lord? "Rosaleen, Luke 16:13 says, 'No servant can serve two masters: for either he will hate the one, and love the other; or else he will hold to the one, and despise the other.' You must decide whether you want to cling to God or to the evils of this world."

He saw her back stiffen. "You *do* think I'm evil!"

"No, of course not. I never said that. . .Rosaleen!" Jacob hated the pride that caused him to remain on the bench and watch her stride up Broadway. He scrubbed his face with his hands then looked down at the stone beneath the willow. "Well, Orville, I really botched that, didn't I?" Because of his own pride he'd pushed her, causing her to turn from making a decision to accept Christ.

Oh God, just give me another chance.

fourteen

"I love that hymn."

At Jacob's quiet voice, Rosaleen's hands stilled on the piano keys in mid-chorus of "There Is a Fountain." Her heart thumping, she turned to face him.

He stood in the parlor doorway, his shoulder leaning against the doorjamb. The tenderness in his eyes took her breath away. "Rosaleen, I'm so sorry I pressured you Sunday." He stepped into the room, his gaze glancing downward, his voice contrite. "I had no right to push you. Accepting Christ into your heart is a very personal thing. I—I only wanted. . ."

"Jacob, I'm sorry, too. I shouldn't have walked away like that." Rising, she hurried to him and touched his arm. How could he imagine he needed to apologize after the gift he'd given her? He'd led her to the verses of scripture that opened her eyes to Christ's love and acceptance. Reading those verses by candlelight on her mattress, she'd run weeping into the open arms of Jesus, inviting His love and salvation into her heart. "Oh Jacob, I have. You made me understand that Jesus does love me. He does accept me, and I've accepted Him."

The tears glistening in Jacob's eyes touched a sweet, deep place in her heart. "Rosaleen, you've made me so happy." His voice thick with emotion, he pulled her into his arms. "The angels in heaven are rejoicing with me. Jesus is rejoicing, too," he murmured against her hair.

Standing in the circle of his arms, she found it easy to imagine staying in Madison. Knowing that Christ had forgiven her sins, she no longer felt dirty, unworthy of Jacob. For the first time, she'd allowed her heart to harbor a tiny glimmer of hope that a future with him might be possible.

His blue eyes seemed to search hers as he pushed gently

away. "I know you have your heart set on going to New York, but I'd like you to reconsider—"

Three quick raps at the front door broke off his sentence.

Reluctantly, Rosaleen wrenched herself away from his embrace. As she left the parlor, Jacob followed her to the front door.

When Rosaleen opened the door, Roscoe Stinnett looked past her shoulder as if she weren't there. "Reverend Hale, I wondered if I might have a few moments of your time."

"Yes, of course, Mr. Stinnett," Jacob replied in a less-than-enthusiastic voice.

Rosaleen answered Jacob's glance of regret with a weak smile. She, too, wished he could have finished his thought a few moments earlier in the parlor. Had he been about to ask her to stay. . .or something more?

After parking Roscoe's gray beaver hat on the hat tree near the front door, Rosaleen went to the dining room and informed Opal of Stinnett's arrival.

Opal walked to the sideboard. "I suppose you'd better offer him some tea and cookies." She began arranging a tea set of her best china on a silver tray. "Personally, I can scarcely abide the man, but he's the wealthiest man in Jacob's congregation, so he must be appeased," she said, placing several ginger cookies on two dessert plates.

Rosaleen picked up the tray and turned toward the kitchen to brew the tea.

"Oh, and Rosaleen," Opal added, halting her at the doorway, "after you attend to Jacob and Mr. Stinnett, would you please make up the beds in the two empty rooms? I hear the *Kentucky Queen* has docked, so we'd better be ready for more boarders."

Rosaleen nodded. The arrival of a steamboat usually meant a full house for the Buchanan Boardinghouse.

A few minutes later, the tray of refreshments in hand, Rosaleen neared the parlor. Roscoe Stinnett's deep voice from inside the room brought her to a sudden stop, causing the china pieces to clink together.

"I'm as eager as you are to get the church built, Reverend," he said. "Why, just the other day, our little Sophie mentioned what a beautiful setting it would be for a fall wedding—the finished brick church with a fine, grand bell tolling the happy event. I'm sure you can appreciate and share that vision."

Jacob's voice stumbled slightly. "Yes, yes of course."

The smile left Stinnett's voice, which hardened to a no-nonsense business tone. "I realize our congregation is small, and the building funds, shall we say, insufficient to expedite the task. I'm prepared to make Sophie's vision of a finished church by September a reality if you are prepared to make the wedding a reality."

Rosaleen's heart stood still then broke at Jacob's quiet response.

"I'd say that would be for the lady to decide."

A numb emptiness filled Rosaleen. How could she have believed, even for one moment, Jacob would prefer her over sweet, pure Sophie? And even if he did, how could she stand in the way of all the dreams he held so dear? If she stayed and Jacob chose her, Stinnett might very well cause a rift in the congregation, jeopardizing Jacob's dream.

"You look like death warmed over!"

Rosaleen jerked at Patsey's voice.

Patsey shook her head and reached for the tray. "Better give me that 'fore you drop it an' smash Mrs. Buchanan's good dishes. Imagine you best go lay down. 'Spect you've got a touch of the ague."

Feeling the strength drain from her limbs, Rosaleen didn't argue with Patsey. Mumbling her thanks, she allowed her friend to take the tray from her limp hands.

Rosaleen knew she should feel happy for Jacob. He'd be getting his church before winter, the bell he had his heart set on, and sweet Sophie for a bride. A host of feelings surged through her, but happiness wasn't one of them.

At the staircase, she swiped at a tear coursing down her

cheek, grasped the balustrade, and started up the steps. One thought formed in her mind as a prayer. *I have to leave Madison. God, help me find a way to leave Madison.*

On the second-story landing, she collided with something solid. Emitting a soft gasp, she found herself engulfed in Alistair's arms.

"You keep runnin' into me like this, and I'll start thinkin' it's on purpose," he said in a teasing tone that sounded superficial.

Pushing away from his grasp, Rosaleen rubbed at the place beneath her throat where Alistair's embrace had caused her brooch to bite into the skin. Like the summer heat lightning that lit the window at the top of the stairway, a sudden thought flashed into her mind. She fingered her mother's brooch and said the words she'd vowed never to say. "Alistair, how much would you pay for my brooch?"

His eyes narrowed. "You'd never sell it before. Why now?"

"I want to leave Madison. I want to go to New York."

"Ah, New York. I haven't been to that city for years." Interest flickered in his gray eyes. "A town ripe for the picking, if memory serves. How 'bout we go together? What do you say?" He reached for her again, but she evaded his grasp. "How much will you give me?" She needed to keep this on a business footing.

"Fifteen dollars."

"No, fifty." He must think she'd learned nothing during her years on the riverboats.

A slow grin crept across his mouth. "You drive a hard bargain, and that's a fact. Your dad would be proud." He cocked his head toward the south wall. "There's a couple fellers on the *Kentucky Queen* who owe me. That's where I'm headed. Let me call in some markers, and I'll get your money."

A blinding flash of lightning and near simultaneous crack of deafening thunder caused her heart to lurch with her body.

"Scared of thunder?" Chuckling softly, he cast a quick

glance at the summer storm brewing outside the little second-story window and clamped one arm around her. With his other hand he touched the jeweled brooch at her bodice, his breath warm against her face. "I can turn this little bauble into enough money to keep us in high style for weeks in New York," he told her in a husky whisper. Slipping both arms around her, he wrapped her in an iron-hard grip. "I like to feel you tremble in my arms."

Panic rose inside Rosaleen when he lowered his head and pressed his lips against the hollow of her throat. He'd abandoned his earlier, casual friendliness. Alistair left no doubt as to his intentions.

She knew she was playing a dangerous game, but the brooch was the only thing of value she owned. Shaken, she twisted from his grip. "Just get the money."

"Eight o'clock next Sunday morning, we can take the *Swiftsure* packet to Cincinnati." He caught her arm, his gaze softening with his voice. "Rosaleen, I wouldn't pay so much if it were anyone else."

Rosaleen watched Alistair descend the stairs. She hated the fact that she'd allowed him to think she would be leaving with him. According to the *Madison Courier*, the packet *Swiftsure* left at eight a.m. every Tuesday, Thursday, and Sunday. Alistair had said Sunday, so she would simply leave the Thursday before—that was, if he got the money to her in time.

Several minutes later, she finished making up the beds as Opal had requested, and still shaky from her exchange with Alistair, Rosaleen went back downstairs. She'd need to find Opal and inform her that the rooms had been prepared. Hearing Opal's voice in the parlor, she walked into the room and studiously ignored Jacob's presence.

Opal stood beside the long front window that rattled from the latest thunderclap. "Fixin' to blow up a real dandy," she said, pulling back the lace curtain to peer at the darkening sky studded with barbs of sharp lightning.

Jacob rose from his desk chair. "Good thing Roscoe left when he did."

Rosaleen stood in the doorway, planning to head for the kitchen as soon as she'd given Opal the information. "The rooms are ready, Opal," she murmured, refusing to look in Jacob's direction. For the next several days she would need to perform a delicate dance, evading both Jacob's questions and Alistair's advances.

Opal let the curtain fall across the window, a look of concern wrinkling her broad brow. "Are you all right, Rosaleen? Patsey said—"

"I'm fine," Rosaleen blurted, eager to get away. The last thing she wanted at the moment was sympathy in any fashion.

Leaving the parlor, Opal said nothing as she passed her in the doorway, but her quizzical look questioned Rosaleen's claim.

Rosaleen turned to follow Opal, but the serious tone in Jacob's voice halted her.

"Rosaleen, I'd like to talk to you."

"The kitchen windows will need to be shut." She mumbled the excuse to leave, poised for a hasty retreat.

Jacob shook his head. "Andrew and Patsey are both in the kitchen, so I'm sure they've already taken care of that."

"I—I. . ." Unable to think of another reason not to stay, she simply turned and started toward the kitchen. Her heart felt unready to hear from Jacob's own lips the news of his engagement to Sophie Schuler.

A banging at the front door turned her around, and she hurried to answer it.

"Is Reverend Hale home?" The wind whipped the black slouch hat Charley Keller twisted in his hands. The worried look drawing hard lines on his face struck Rosaleen's heart with fear. She knew that Charley, a member of Jacob's congregation, belonged to the Fair Play Volunteer Fire Company.

"What is it, Charley?" From behind her, the fear tightening Jacob's voice echoed her own.

"It's the church, Reverend. Lightning struck it. We have a bucket brigade goin' from the river but. . ." The helpless look in his eyes conveyed his grim prediction.

fifteen

Opal gasped and Jacob's face went paper white.

Bolting out the open door, he leaped from the porch and raced up Mulberry Street toward Main-Cross, Charley Keller at his heels.

Dread squeezed Rosaleen's throat as she and Opal watched from the porch until Jacob disappeared at the junction of Main-Cross and Mulberry. "I think we need to pray, Opal." She slipped a trembling arm around Mrs. Buchanan. Together, they walked inside to join the Chapmans in the kitchen.

Outside, the winds wailed, and leaves from the bowing ash and oak trees blew past the kitchen window.

Opal arranged four chairs in a crude circle and asked Andrew to lead them in prayer.

Rosaleen slumped to the seat of a kitchen chair, her tears mimicking the rain sheeting down the windowpane. The image of Jacob's church—his dream—consumed by flames gouged at her heart. *Why, God? Why?* How could God do this to such a good man? A man who'd worked so hard for Him. The man who never gave up on her but helped bring her to the salvation of Christ. The man she loved. Her heart ached, remembering the pride in his face as he'd gazed at the unfinished church.

Andrew sat with his head bowed, his arms resting on the tops of his legs and his fingers laced together. "We don't know Yer mind, Lord. But we 'cept Yer will and rest in Yer promises."

As Andrew prayed, Rosaleen remembered a scripture from the Gospel of John she'd read the night before. "*Jesus answered, Neither hath this man sinned, nor his parents: but that the works of God should be made manifest in him.*"

How could this tragedy glorify God? Perhaps the rain had put out the fire, saving the church.

Hours later, Rosaleen realized there'd been no such miracle. Long after the Chapmans had left for home and Opal had gone to bed, Rosaleen could not bring herself to climb up to her attic room while still unsure of Jacob's safety. Regardless of her earlier resolve to avoid him, she could not abandon him tonight.

She sat at the piano, softly playing "Rock of Ages" by the flickering light of a single lamp. The jingle of the front doorbell halted her fingers.

Jacob trudged slump shouldered into the parlor, bringing with him the smell of wood smoke. The despair on his soot-streaked face confirmed her fears. "It's gone." With those two words, he walked to his desk, pulled out the chair, and sank to the seat, a vacant look in his blue eyes.

"Oh Jacob, I'm so sorry." Choking back tears, she rushed to him, knelt at his feet, and took his sooty hands into her own.

"Was it my pride, Rosaleen? Was I too prideful about the church? Or is God just trying to tell me I'm not called to preach?"

Though her heart wept for his loss, Rosaleen's love for Jacob wouldn't allow her to sit mutely by as he turned his back on his dream of preaching in a church he'd helped to build.

"Not called? Jacob, it's because of your preaching, your guidance, that I sought Jesus. How can you believe God hasn't called you?"

"I just can't believe it's happened again." As she'd seen him do many times, he absently touched the scar on his left cheek. She'd wondered about the scar but had never asked.

"Is that how you got that. . .in a fire?"

"My family's barn burned when I was sixteen. When I went into the barn to chase out the livestock, I was burned by a piece of hot metal on a harness.

Smiling, she reached up and traced the raised scar on his cheek with her fingertip. "I've always found it attractive."

Love bubbled up inside Rosaleen as she imagined the young Jacob's bravery during his family's tragedy. "Did God restore your barn?"

Even in the dim light and beneath all the soot, she saw Jacob's face flush at her touch. "Yes, the community raised us a new one." His mouth lifted in a wry smile. "But that was just a barn, Rosaleen, not a church."

Rosaleen gave Jacob's fingers a little squeeze and willed him to look into her eyes. "Jacob, that night when the *Cortland Belle* caught fire, before I knew God loved me, I'd considered drowning myself. But when the fire forced me into the river, something inside me wouldn't let me die. I know now that it was God, saving me so you could bring me to His Son. You told me Christ doesn't reject anyone. It is people who reject Him." She cupped the side of his face in her hand. "I'm a perfect example that God doesn't give up on us. So we shouldn't give up on Him, right? If God restored your barn, I'm sure He will restore your church."

His eyes shimmered with tears in the dim lamplight. Rising, he gripped her hands and helped her to her feet. "You are amazing," he murmured.

Her heart pounding, she stood immobile, held captive as his gaze melted into hers and he drew her into his arms. Melding into his smoke-scented embrace, she welcomed his kiss with a fervor that matched his own. Half believing it was all a beautiful dream, Rosaleen prayed it would never end. She wanted to stay here forever in the arms of her beloved "angel."

In one swift movement, he knelt before her on one knee. "Rosaleen, I love you with all my heart, and I'll need you for the rest of my life. I don't think I can manage without you. Will you please do me the honor of becoming my wife?"

Her heart full to bursting with joy, she gazed down into his dear face through a mist of tears. At first she could only nod, emotion choking her voice. "Yes," she finally managed to squeeze through a sob. "Yes, yes, yes—" She couldn't stop saying the word until he stood, pulled her into his arms, and pressed his lips against hers once more.

A troubling thought intruded into her beautiful dream, and she pulled away from him. "But what about Sophie? I thought you and Sophie. . . I overheard Mr. Stinnett this afternoon. He said he'd pay for your church, even the bell, if you and Sophie. . ." She couldn't bring herself to finish the sentence.

"Darling"—smiling, he cradled her in his arms—"what Roscoe proposed would not be fair to either Sophie or me. Sophie deserves a man who loves her. I don't love her—not that way. I love you. You are the woman I want to be my wife." He grinned. "Besides, from what I understand, Sophie has a constant bevy of suitors. Roscoe Stinnett has no right to choose a husband for his niece."

Rosaleen could not so easily dismiss the concerns dulling her joy. She pulled away again. "But, Jacob, you need Mr. Stinnett's offer more now than before. What if he becomes angry and causes you trouble?"

"Sweet Rosaleen." Jacob drew her back into his arms. "You just reminded me not to limit God. If my church is to be, God will find a way."

Even as Rosaleen snuggled against Jacob, unease gripped her heart, choking her happiness. What if God had provided Roscoe Stinnett's offer as an antidote to the church fire? What if her selfish desire to marry Jacob denied him the church and congregation he had his heart set on?

Oh God, why can't things be simple? Please don't let this cause Jacob trouble.

&

"What you grinnin' like a 'possum about?" Patsey asked the next morning as she walked through the kitchen door, a basket of freshly picked okra on her arm.

Smiling, Rosaleen glanced up from rolling piecrust on the floured table. She'd decided to make Jacob's favorite, blackberry pie, for supper to celebrate their engagement.

Enveloped in the sweet euphoria of her beautiful dream, Rosaleen could scarcely believe the events of the night before.

Though still worried about potential repercussions of her engagement to Jacob, she'd decided to trust God and bask in her happiness.

Patsey narrowed suspicious eyes at Rosaleen, her brow scrunched. Her words slowed to a thoughtful crawl. "Come to think on it, the rev'rend seemed unusual happy this mornin', considerin' the church burnin' an' all."

"Jacob asked me to marry him last night," Rosaleen blurted. She'd planned to keep it a secret for a while and hadn't even told Opal yet, but she felt her heart might burst with the news if she didn't free it.

Dropping the basket of okra onto the washstand, a wide-eyed Patsey screeched. Waddling around the table, she hurried to her. "I knowed it, I knowed it, I knowed it!" She hugged Rosaleen as tightly as her extended belly would allow. "When?"

"We haven't set a date yet."

"This time next year, yer li'ble to be in the same shape as me." Patsey patted her belly.

"Patsey!" Though heat flooded her face, Rosaleen couldn't help grinning at her friend's excitement.

"I can jis see our young'uns playin' on the floor together." Patsey seemed compelled to give her another hug. As she embraced her, she whispered, "Another train's comin' tonight. Crossin' the river 'bout midnight. Need every willin' hand to help. Can you meet me and Andrew behind the boardinghouse after dark?"

Rosaleen nodded. It would be harder now to keep such things from Jacob. She knew he would approve of her work with the Underground Railroad, yet she felt the need to protect him from such knowledge just as Andrew and Patsey protected one another. Rafe Arbuckle, or worse, the sheriff, might come to question him again.

ᝨ

Later that afternoon in the parlor, Rosaleen had to think what Alistair meant when he said, "I have your money."

Remembering their deal, she fingered her brooch. There was no need for her to sell it now, or was there? This morning, it had pained her to see Jacob's glum face when he returned from the bank. He'd been unsuccessful in procuring a loan for more lumber, and a look of dejection had clouded his eyes as he left the boardinghouse to help clear away the charred remains of the church.

Alistair pulled five ten-dollar notes from his vest pocket. "C'mon, love. A deal's a deal." At her hesitation, he held out his hand. With impatient movements, he curled his fingers toward his palm.

Blinking back tears, she removed the brooch, placed it in his hand, and accepted the money.

Oh God, please let this buy lots of lumber for the church.

Rosaleen planned to surprise Jacob with the money at supper. But long after the supper table had been cleared, he dragged himself into the boardinghouse kitchen. The exhaustion and defeat in his face as he collapsed to a caned chair at the little kitchen table ripped at her heart. He seemed almost too tired to eat the cold chicken, fried okra, and black-berry pie she placed before him.

He looked up at her, his eyes full of regret, his weary face and blond hair streaked with the soot of yesterday's fire. "I'm sorry, darling. Opal told me you made the pie to celebrate our engagement. But we're halfway through July, and there's not a minute to lose. I'd sure like for us to be married in that church before the snow flies."

"What about your bell money?" The money from her brooch wouldn't come close to what he needed, but it would double the money he'd saved.

He gave her a sad smile. "I know it sounds irrational. What use is a bell if there's no church, right? Yet I can't seem to bring myself to spend it on lumber."

"God will provide, Jacob. In fact, He has." She dipped her hand into her pocket, her fingers curling around what now represented her mother's brooch.

Standing, he yawned and rubbed his hand over his drawn features. "Please, Rosaleen, let's talk about it in the morning. I'm just too tired right now." He brushed a kiss across her lips then plodded from the kitchen.

Rosaleen drew her hand from her pocket. Perhaps it was best this way. Maybe after a good night's rest, Jacob would be more apt to view her offering as a blessing rather than a pitiful fraction of what he required.

That night, she tucked the money deep amid her mattress's straw stuffing then stole quietly out to meet the Chapmans.

Pink streaks of dawn stained the eastern horizon by the time Rosaleen parted with Patsey and Andrew and slipped quietly into the kitchen door of the boardinghouse. She'd spent the past several hours near the river's edge assisting the Chapmans and others connected with the Underground Railroad. Mostly, she'd helped dispense food, water, and dry blankets to a dozen or so brave souls who'd managed to cross the river at a shallow point under cover of darkness. Although exhausted, Rosaleen felt good about her nocturnal endeavors. She'd even assisted Andrew in bandaging the wound of a young man who'd been shot while fleeing slave hunters.

In her dark room, she changed into her nightdress and collapsed to her mattress.

Her next conscious sensation was warmth bathing her face. She opened her eyes, blinking against the bright morning sun flooding through the little window above her. Jumping up from her mattress, Rosaleen realized she'd overslept.

Her fingers flew as she threw on and buttoned up the dress she'd worn the night before. She stuffed the fifty dollars Alistair had paid her for the brooch into the pocket of her skirt. After breakfast, she would walk to the church site and surprise Jacob with the money.

Downstairs, she glanced through the parlor doorway and caught a glimpse of Jacob's blond head bent over the mahogany desk. She was glad to see he hadn't yet left for the church and prayed that her surprise would help cheer him up.

"Jacob," she whispered, reluctant to disturb his prayer time. She took a tentative step into the parlor.

He raised his head but didn't look at her. Something in his demeanor caused her heart to quake.

"Jacob?"

He sat motionless, an unspeakable anguish veiling his blue eyes.

Assuming his attitude was caused by his despondency over the ruined church, she pulled the bank notes from her pocket. "I want you to have this—to buy lumber for the church."

He sprang from the chair, knocking it backward, sending Rosaleen's blood sluicing to her toes. The muscles worked in his jaw as if straining to hold in check the anger smoldering in his eyes.

When at last he spoke, the words he ground through his clenched jaw shredded her heart. "How can you imagine I'd want your dirty money?"

sixteen

Jacob's heart throbbed with exquisite agony as Rosaleen smiled and thrust a fistful of ten-dollar notes toward him. Then anger—blessed, blessed anger—surged through him, anesthetizing the pain. "Where's your brooch?"

"I—I sold it."

His eyes closed against the lie. Her offering confirmed the truth his mind and heart had rebelled against since Constable Rafe Arbuckle's visit just after dawn. What the constable told him when he handed him Rosaleen's brooch had frozen Jacob's heart to his ribs.

A knife fight had broken out during a card game at the Billiard Saloon. A man had been stabbed, but no one either could or would identify him. The participants of the game had skedaddled just before the lawmen arrived.

Rafe said he'd found Rosaleen's brooch among the money abandoned on the gambling table. Having remembered seeing her wear it, Rafe had brought it by, figuring it had either been lost or stolen.

Somehow Jacob forced his gaze to meet Rosaleen's. "Where were you last night, and how did you get that blood on your dress?" Though he realized it was useless to interrogate her, he couldn't seem to help himself.

"What?" She glanced down at her stained skirt and gasped. Obviously she hadn't realized her clothes bore the evidence of last night's escapades.

Her wide eyes held the look of a trapped animal. "I—I—"

"No, don't lie." He held his palm out toward her as she opened her mouth. Jacob couldn't help wondering if she'd truly experienced a conversion. He should have realized her life on the riverboats would equip her with the skills of an

111

actress. Could he even trust anything she'd told him? There was no way to discern the lies from the truth.

"There is evidence that you were gambling at the Billiard Saloon last night. A man was stabbed, but then you know that." His gaze settled on her incriminating bloodstained skirt.

"You'd believe that about me?"

He steeled himself against the tears streaming down her face. *She's acting*, he admonished his melting heart. "The evidence is before my eyes!"

"If you can think such a thing of me, then I can never be your wife." She choked the words through realistic sobs.

"That, Mrs. Archer—if that indeed is your name, may be the most truthful statement you've made to me thus far."

As she fled the room in tears, he reached down and righted his chair then sank to its seat. Opening the desk drawer, he gazed for a moment at the gold and rose quartz cameo framed by tiny pearls and rubies—the brooch Rosaleen had pretended she cared so much about.

Had her conversion—the event that had made him believe again in his calling—been nothing but a farce, a sham? How could he now ignore God's voice telling him he was not fit for the ministry? He slammed the drawer shut, feeling as if his heart had been hollowed out.

Sitting numbly, Jacob stirred at the sound of the front doorbell.

Quiet murmurings and sniffling sounds emanated from the front hallway before Opal ushered Sophie Schuler into the parlor.

"Oh Jacob, you must help me. I—I don't know what to do." Sophie's little face crumpled, and her words dissolved into sobs. She rustled toward him in a dress of pale yellow silk that nearly matched the curls dangling at the sides of her face. Always struck by her small stature, he thought she'd never looked more doll-like.

"Sophie, dear, whatever is wrong?" He gathered his friend into his arms.

This must be the day for broken hearts.

"It's Uncle Roscoe."

"Is your uncle ill?" Jacob guided her to the settee. Pulling a calico work kerchief from his back pocket, he offered it to the distraught girl.

"No, his health is fine. He's just stubborn." She stamped her little foot on the carpeted floor. "It concerns Edwin, Edwin Applegate." She dabbed at her reddened eyes with the piece of calico. "Edwin and I have come to love each other very much," she managed between sniffs. "He has declared his devotion to me but is afraid to ask Uncle Roscoe for my hand."

Sophie's revelation caught Jacob off guard. He knew she'd become very friendly with the Applegate twins and that her uncle was less than pleased with that fact. However, embroiled in his own concerns of the heart, he'd had no idea she and Edwin Applegate had developed a romantic relationship. He had to assume Roscoe suspected such an alliance. Her uncle's attempt to coerce him into asking for Sophie's hand began to make sense.

Learning that Sophie had situated her heart upon Edwin Applegate brought Jacob a measure of relief. Though heartbroken and disappointed by Rosaleen, he had no intention of marrying a girl he did not love.

Feeling an affinity with his childhood friend's heartache, he strove to comfort her. "Your uncle's dispute is with Edwin's father, not Edwin. Perhaps you might ease him into the idea gradually. Have Edwin come to court you."

"That's just it. . ." A new wave of sobs shook her. Then, with a ragged breath, she seemed to compose herself. "Uncle Roscoe won't allow anyone by the name of Applegate anywhere near the house. Aunt Myrtle sympathizes and likes Edwin, but she loathes discord above all else and will not bring up the subject. Neither Papa nor my brother, Will, is here to help me, and I simply did not know where else to turn."

"Couldn't you write to your family for support?"

"Of course. But not knowing Edwin, they'd defer to Uncle

Roscoe. You know they would." This admission brought with it a fresh gush of tears. "Oh, Jacob, you must intercede. Uncle Roscoe will listen to you. He will. He must." She daintily blew her nose on the kerchief.

"Yes, of course, Sophie." He took her lace-gloved hands into his. "You know I will do all that is in my power to see to your happiness." Meeting her shaky smile with his steady one, Jacob wondered if God had allowed his heartache so that he might better understand Sophie's.

"Oh, thank you, Jacob!" She wrapped her arms around his neck and kissed his cheek.

Jacob prayed for a happier conclusion to Sophie's romance than he'd experienced with his own.

❧

After changing her bloody skirt for a clean one, Rosaleen started down the stairs. She'd fled the parlor, hurt by the fact that Jacob had been so quick to believe she'd patronized the seedy Billiard Saloon. After several minutes of cool reflection, however, she realized that her past, the bloodstains on her skirt, and her lack of another explanation might cause him to wonder.

Yet he had said there was *evidence* she'd been there. What evidence? Had Alistair claimed she'd been there with him? But then, she could not imagine Jacob believing Alistair or that Alistair would even make such a claim.

Only two nights ago, Jacob had asked her to be his wife. Surely he would believe her if she explained. Since Rafe Arbuckle had already questioned Jacob about the runaways, he'd most likely not question him again.

Unwilling to allow her and Jacob's love—their future together—to be unraveled by a misunderstanding, Rosaleen headed back to the parlor, anxious to mend the rift in their relationship.

What she saw when she reached the parlor doorway drained her blood to her toes. Jacob and Sophie Schuler stood entwined in each other's arms. She heard Jacob promising in tender tones to see to Sophie's happiness.

Stunned to numbness, Rosaleen turned and walked back to the stairway.

At the second-story hallway, she gazed out the window. Tears filled her eyes, obscuring the image of the couple in the open landau below her. She watched Jacob and Sophie drive away, and her beautiful dream evaporated, distilled into bitter tears that slid down her face.

Jacob had wasted no time accepting Roscoe Stinnett's offer, it would seem.

Anger replaced the numbness, salving Rosaleen's wounded heart. She fingered the bills in her skirt pocket. At least she still had the money from the brooch. Tomorrow was Thursday, so she could leave for Cincinnati on the packet *Swiftsure*. If she exercised some care, the fifty dollars might even get her all the way to New York.

As she headed for the stairs that led to her attic room, she heard what sounded like a low moan. It came from Alistair's room. Curious, she stopped. "Alistair, are you all right?"

"Go away." A fit of coughing followed his strained reply.

"Alistair, if you're ill. . ." When she heard another moan in response, Rosaleen opened the door.

Alistair lay drenched with sweat, still in the clothes he'd worn the day before. A deep maroon stain covered the left side of his chest.

Jacob's words slammed to the front of Rosaleen's mind. "Alistair, did this happen at the Billiard Saloon?"

"Yeah, little weasel accused me of cheating."

"Were you cheating?

"Maybe." His grin twisted into a grimace. " 'Fraid I lost your brooch," he said, squeezing the words between groans as Rosaleen worked to gently remove his jacket and shirt.

"You didn't tell Reverend Hale that I was with you, did you?"

He swore beneath his breath as she extricated his arms from his bloody sleeves. " 'Course not. Ain't seen the good rev'rend."

She gasped at the ugly red wound just below his left collarbone. His assailant had obviously been aiming for Alistair's heart. She sent a silent prayer of thanks heavenward that the man's aim had been poor. The fact that Alistair had managed to walk the distance from the riverfront to the boardinghouse in this condition testified to his considerable constitution. He'd need it all if he were to ultimately survive the assault, she realized.

She examined the inflamed area around his wound. It felt hot to her touch. "I need to get Dr. Morgan."

"No." He clutched her hand, his gray eyes wild with fear and fever. "No doctor. But if you'd see to me I'd be obliged." A fresh spate of coughing followed his labored words. "Please. I helped your dad once, remember, Rosaleen? Could you help me, for old times' sake?" With each coughing fit, more blood trickled from the wound on his chest.

Her heart softened at the memory of Alistair standing between her consumptive father and the man who'd intended to thrash him after a card game went sour. "Of course I'll help you, Alistair. But you're very ill. You need a doctor."

"Doctors ask questions," he said with a painful-sounding gasp. "Can't take the chance. Don't think I'll be in any shape to leave Sunday, either."

"Just lie still. I'll take care of you." Although unscrupulous and flawed, Alistair was an old friend. Looking down at his features reconfigured with pain as he lay wounded— perhaps mortally—she knew she could not desert him.

Rosaleen's heart fell. She wouldn't be taking the packet to Cincinnati any time soon.

seventeen

"Sure wish you were here, old friend." Jacob shoved his fingers through his hair and dropped to the bench beside Orville's grave.

His meeting with Roscoe Stinnett had been, at least in part, successful. Roscoe had grudgingly agreed to allow young Edwin Applegate to court Sophie on the condition that she would not promise herself to him immediately.

Though not entirely happy with the compromise, Sophie had grasped her uncle's proffered olive branch. Later, she intimated to Jacob that she felt confident she'd soon persuade her uncle to bless her and Edwin's engagement.

Walking back from the Stinnetts', Jacob's conscience chafed. Perhaps he'd been too hasty in his judgment of Rosaleen. Needing to sort out his jumbled feelings concerning the woman he loved, he'd gone to the place where he communed most closely with the Lord.

Oh God, show me what You'd have me do. If it is impossible for our lives to merge, then why has my heart twined so tightly around hers?

He gazed up at the charred debris that would have been the new church. As he remembered her sweet encouragements, regret smote his heart. As a new Christian, she couldn't be expected to cast away her old life so easily. Her heart had been in the right place; she'd simply gone about it all wrong. She knew he needed money. And he could see how, having learned to gamble at her father's knee, she might turn to the gaming table as a way to procure quick cash.

He also realized his initial anger had been caused by the vision of Rosaleen spending an evening gambling in the company of Alistair Ralston. Somewhere in a deep, ugly little corner of his heart, suspicions concerning her relationship with the gambler still festered. But if she loved Alistair, and not him, why would she have offered the money for the church instead of simply leaving with the man?

Jacob scrubbed his face with his hand. He gazed out over the river dotted with barges and flatboats—many arriving with merchandise from all corners of the world. Rosaleen, too, had come from the river. And just like the items on these boats, she'd come from a place—a life—far different from his.

Remembering the pain in Rosaleen's eyes at his hateful rejection of her offered money, Jacob winced. Shame bowed his head. *I even questioned her sincerity in accepting Christ!*

He'd failed her. As a minister, it was his place to guide her, to help her grow in her new Christian life. Instead, he'd flung accusations at her, giving her no chance to explain. Whether or not they should ever marry did not change the fact that he loved her. He would always love her, and now he'd shirked his duty in ministering to her.

The scripture he'd quoted earlier to Roscoe Stinnett from Luke 6:37 echoed through his anguished mind, convicting him of his own shortcomings: *"Judge not, and ye shall not be judged: condemn not, and ye shall not be condemned: forgive, and ye shall be forgiven."*

For weeks he'd been teaching her of Christ's message of forgiveness, but when tested, he'd failed to forgive her.

At the sound of a steamboat's whistle, he turned toward the Ohio. Gazing at the white riverboat with its huge scarlet paddle wheel at the stern, his eyes misted.

God, is that why You allowed me to fall in love with someone who came from a life so different from my own? Are You testing my willingness to forgive?

His heart and mind in turmoil, he walked down to Ohio Street then east toward Mulberry. As he passed the Billiard Saloon, he fought anger and pain. He could imagine the woman he loved—the woman he'd asked to be his wife— gambling beside Alistair Ralston.

By the time he'd reached the Newell Carriage Company at the junction of Mulberry and Second Street, Jacob knew he needed to talk to Becky and Ephraim. Perhaps they'd be better able to help him put it all in perspective.

When he came to the intersection of Mulberry and Main-Cross, he turned west and walked to the home of his sister and brother-in-law.

"Oh Jacob, come in. I am so sorry about the church." Becky gave him a warm hug as she ushered him inside.

What a comfort to feel his sister's arms around him. "Thanks, sis, but that's not why I'm here."

"What's the matter?" Becky's blue eyes, which so mirrored his own, filled with concern. She guided him toward the parlor.

Daniel bounded into the room, hope lighting his little face. "Uncle Jacob, will you take me fishing down at the river?"

Jacob gave his nephew a weak smile. He hated disappointing Daniel, but right now he needed Becky's counsel. "Sorry, Daniel. Next week, I promise."

"Daniel, go get that basket by the back door and pick a nice big mess of green beans from the garden for supper, please." Becky smiled at her son's sour expression. "And don't pick them too small," she added as he headed toward the kitchen.

When the back door slammed shut, she turned again to Jacob. "Is it Rosaleen?"

Sinking uninvited to the seat of a wing chair, Jacob felt a wry grin pull at his mouth. "How do you always know these things?"

Becky sat opposite him on the sofa. "I know the look of heartbreak when I see it. What's happened?"

He blew out a long sigh. "I thought I knew her, Becky. I was so sure she cared for me. So sure she'd given her heart to Christ. How could I have been so wrong—as a man and as a minister?" He raised his shoulders in a defeated shrug. "I'm seriously doubting that I'm fit for the ministry. . .or if I should even rebuild the church."

"Jacob, if you don't tell me this minute what's happened, I'm going to shake you!"

"She gambled down at the Billiard Saloon with that Ralston character then had the gall to offer me the money she'd won to help rebuild the church." Hurt and anger hardened his words.

Ephraim entered the parlor, a frown wrinkling his brow. "Excuse me for intruding, but I overheard some of what you were telling Becky. When do you believe Rosaleen was at the saloon?"

Jacob turned to face his brother-in-law. "Last night. Rafe Arbuckle brought her brooch by this morning. There was some kind of ruckus down at the Billiard Saloon last night. A gambler was supposedly stabbed during a card game, but all the players took off before Rafe got there. He found Rosaleen's brooch on the table where the fight took place."

Jacob hated the tears that sprang to his eyes when he recounted how Rosaleen had offered him fifty dollars this morning to help rebuild the church. He swallowed past the painful knot in his throat and fixed his brother-in-law with a hard stare. "Ephraim, I saw blood on the front of her skirt. What am I supposed to think?"

"I don't know how her brooch came to be at the Billiard Saloon, but she wasn't there. Not last night, anyway." Ephraim's voice slowed as he joined Becky on the settee, sliding his arm around his wife.

Jacob prayed Ephraim was right. "How do you know?"

Becky and Ephraim exchanged a long, knowing look, and Becky gave her husband a little nod.

Ephraim turned back to face Jacob. "Because she was down at the river with Andrew and Patsey, helping people come across."

"The Underground?" It had never crossed Jacob's mind that Rosaleen might have become involved in that work.

Ephraim nodded. "Andrew sent word this morning, asking me to stop by their house. I assumed it was to check on Patsey."

He went on to explain that when he arrived at the Chapmans', he found a young runaway slave who'd been shot in the shoulder. The doctor's lips tipped in a reassuring smile. "Andrew told me how Rosaleen helped him bandage the fellow when he came out of the river bleeding."

"She's been doing this, helping with the Underground?" Stunned, Jacob sat straight up.

"Yes." His brother-in-law hesitated before continuing. "I'm not at liberty to divulge any particulars, but I know she's been involved in several instances."

As much as he wanted to believe Rosaleen innocent of the happenings at the saloon, Jacob had to know for sure. "Maybe she was at the Billiard before she went to Georgetown?"

"Did Rafe say what time the altercation occurred?" Ephraim asked.

"About midnight."

Ephraim shook his head. "According to Andrew, Rosaleen was with them from about nine thirty last night until nearly dawn this morning."

Relief washed over Jacob.

Ephraim's smile broadened. "She obviously got the blood on her dress while helping to bandage that young man's wound."

Jacob groaned. A smothering wave of regret doused his joy at Rosaleen's exoneration. "You say she's helped with the Underground before?" That could explain the nocturnal sounds of comings and goings emanating from her third-floor attic room.

Ephraim nodded. "According to Andrew, yes."

"Jacob"—Becky's eyes were kind, her voice gentle as she took his hand—"talk to her. Get it all aired out. Don't let your pride get in God's way. And whatever you do, don't jump to any more conclusions."

Riddled with remorse, Jacob hurried back to the boarding-house. He prayed that somehow Rosaleen could find it in her heart to forgive him.

When he arrived, he poked his head into the kitchen.

"Opal, have you seen Rosaleen?"

His landlady turned from stirring a pot of beans on the stove. "I think she's upstairs." She gave him a questioning look. "Have you two had a spat? I thought I saw her crying earlier."

"Something like that, yes." Jacob forced a weak smile. He knew Mrs. Buchanan meant well, but he was in no mood to share the particulars of his and Rosaleen's difficulties.

While he passed Alistair Ralston's room, the sound of Rosaleen's voice stopped Jacob.

"Shh, Alistair. I promise I won't leave you." Her tender words, followed by deep moans and the creaking of a mattress moving, froze Jacob's blood.

The image forming in Jacob's mind cleaved his heart. With Herculean effort, he restrained himself from flinging open the door, revealing their shame.

What a fool he'd been. His desire for reconciliation with Rosaleen disintegrated as he flew down the steps.

eighteen

"Alistair, you must allow me to call Dr. Morgan." Rosaleen supported the back of his head and held a glass of water to his parched lips.

"No. I'll live or I'll die here, but I won't die on the floor of some jailhouse," he said, pushing the glass away.

Gently lifting the cotton bandage from his chest, she gasped at the putrid-smelling wound oozing pus. "Dr. Morgan won't turn you over to the sheriff, I promise you."

He grasped her wrist, his feverish gray eyes glistening with tears. "Rosaleen, the only promise I ask is that you, alone, will tend to me."

Rosaleen hesitated. She would do what she could to help Alistair, but she wouldn't lie for him. "All right, but I don't know how much longer I can keep your condition from Mrs. Buchanan, Patsey. . .or Jacob." Her voice caught at the thought of the man she loved. In the two days since their confrontation in the parlor, she'd seen very little of Jacob.

Opal's and Patsey's subdued attitudes suggested they sensed the rift in Rosaleen and Jacob's relationship. But respecting the couple's privacy, the two women had said nothing.

Rosaleen simply told them she needed to attend to her friend, Alistair, who was under the weather—an expression they'd translate as having drank too much.

As discreetly as possible, she'd carried bandages and fresh water to his room, but she had nothing to combat the deadly fever.

"At least allow me to get a bottle of that Smith's Tonic Syrup fever remedy Maynard's Apothecary has been advertising in the *Madison Courier*."

"All right." He seemed too weak to argue. "Look in my

123

vest pocket. There's some money." As usual, too many words precipitated a coughing fit.

"Don't talk. I'll get it." She dipped a piece of cloth into the washbowl, wrung it out, and gently dabbed his mouth.

God, don't let him die. I've seen enough death. And maybe—just maybe—I can bring him to You.

She peeled a dollar from the folded bills in his vest pocket and could not help shaking her head. *Such a little bit of money couldn't have been worth risking your life for, Alistair.*

Assured that Alistair was again resting easy, Rosaleen left to purchase the medicine.

"Rosaleen."

As she closed Alistair's door behind her, Rosaleen jerked at Jacob's soft voice.

"I need to talk to you." There was a cool formality to his tone.

"I—I have to get something for Alistair." She couldn't bear another scathing diatribe from Jacob.

"This will only take a moment." His demeanor seemed more contrite than condemning. "I owe you an apology." His gaze avoided hers. "I was wrong to accuse you the other day. I've since learned from Ephraim that you were not at the Billiard Saloon the other night." He reached into his pocket. What he produced caused her eyes to widen.

"My brooch! Where did you get it?"

"Constable Arbuckle found it at the Billiard Saloon. I should have given it to you days ago." His penitent words seemed at odds with his stiff tone. "I'm sorry. I have no excuse for my actions."

Rosaleen paused, waiting for him to ask her to reinstate their engagement. When he didn't, disappointment surged through her. She shook her head. "It's no longer mine. I sold it to Alistair. . .for money to go to New York." Her voice faltered as she remembered Jacob's angry rejection of that money.

To his credit, a look of surprise registered on his face,

followed by something akin to shame. "You're still going, then?" His voice tightening, he looked everywhere but in her eyes.

"Yes." Her voice caught on the word. She could see no reason to stay. Jacob would soon be marrying Sophie. As fond as Rosaleen was of Sophie, she couldn't bear to stay and watch it happen.

"Guess I should give this to Mr. Ralston, then," he said.

Tears sprang to her eyes as she watched Jacob hold in his open palm the piece of jewelry she'd treasured all her life.

"He's—he's not been feeling well for the past couple of days." She stumbled, not wanting to lie, yet at the same time, trying to keep Alistair's injury secret. "Would you please keep it until he's better?"

"Of course." A hint of a smile?

Brushing past him, she fled down the stairs. Alistair needed the fever medicine, and Jacob Hale's nearness inflicted far more torture on her heart than Rosaleen cared to endure.

৵

Jacob started toward his room but stopped at the door. He gazed at the jeweled pin in his hand. It reminded him of his love for Rosaleen. No matter what her relationship with Alistair Ralston, Jacob knew he would always love her. Why should he keep this reminder of his loss a minute longer than necessary? If Ralston had a throbbing head from drinking whiskey down at the Billiard Saloon, that was just too bad.

"Mr. Ralston? Mr. Ralston?" He rapped twice on the man's door. Getting no reply, he pushed it open. What he saw set him back on his heels.

"Go away! She said she wouldn't tell." Ralston reared up then fell heavily back onto the pillow, coughing.

Like a lightning bolt, the larger reality shot through Jacob. Ralston must have been the man knifed down at the Billiard. "You're in a bad way, man."

Jacob walked to the bed where Ralston lay shirtless, a bloodstained bandage covering his chest. He realized, too, that what he'd imagined happening between Rosaleen and Alistair two days ago could not have been possible. Jacob's groans echoed those of the wounded man on the bed. "Rosaleen never told me. She only said you weren't feeling well. I supposed you'd just had too much to drink."

"You won't tell anybody about my. . .accident, will you, Rev'rend?" Fear flickered in the big gambler's eyes.

Jacob glanced at the bloody bandage covering the man's chest. "I won't tell if you don't want me to, but if a doctor doesn't attend you soon it won't matter. You'll be dead."

"There was a bit of a misunderstandin' down at the Billiard a couple nights ago. I don't want to go to jail—" A wheezing cough swallowed Ralston's words.

Jacob lifted the bandage. "My brother-in-law is a doctor. Ephraim won't tell the sheriff. He'll simply tend to you." The look of relief on the man's face sparked sympathy in Jacob.

Tension seeped out of the man's ashen features. "All right, but would you promise me something, Rev'rend?"

"Sure."

"I—I don't have much, but if I die, would you see to it that Rosaleen gets everything?"

"Yes, of course." Jacob gave the man a small smile. "I've seen men in worse shape make it." He hoped his voice carried more conviction than he felt. "Would you like me to pray for you?"

Alistair's soft chuckle turned to a series of coughs. "Sure, Rev'rend. Rosaleen's been prayin' over me for two days. Maybe somethin' will get through, huh?"

"It all gets through, my friend," Jacob said, patting the man's shoulder. After offering up a prayer for Alistair, Jacob added a silent prayer, asking God's forgiveness for misjudging Rosaleen.

"I believe I have something of yours, Mr. Ralston." Jacob fished in the pocket of his trousers and pulled out the brooch. "Rosaleen tells me she sold this to you some days ago."

"Yeah." Alistair's eyes grew wide and, with a deep groan, he pushed up to a sitting position.

"Was this still in your possession when you left the gambling table?" If he'd lost it in the game, Jacob would hand it back to Rafe Arbuckle to put in the sheriff's sale.

"Yeah. I'd just thrown it into the pot, but it was still mine. I never got the chance to finish the hand."

"You swear that's the truth?"

"That's the truth, Rev'rend."

"Then I'd like to buy it from you." Jacob didn't blame Rosaleen for hating him. He'd accused her without allowing her an opportunity to explain. He didn't deserve her love or her forgiveness, nor did he expect them. The thought skewered his heart. He could never make up for how he'd treated her, but he *could* do this for her. "How much did you pay her for it?"

Alistair glanced down at the patchwork quilt. "Seventy-five dollars."

A quick anger replaced the sympathy Jacob had felt for the man. Rosaleen had offered him fifty, and his heart told him she would have offered all she had. "This is no time for a ruse, Ralston," he growled. "I'll give you fifty."

"Fifty will do."

Jacob walked to his room and reached under his bed for the tattered cigar box. A feeling of gratitude washed over him. Perhaps this was why he'd resisted spending his bell money even after the church burned.

Thank You, Jesus, for whispering to me not to spend this on new lumber.

Back in Alistair's room, Jacob counted out the money. "Fifty dollars."

"Put it in my vest pocket." Ralston rammed a thumb toward his gold brocade vest draped across the back of a wing chair.

Jacob stuffed the bills into the showy piece of apparel then turned back to the man. "Mr. Ralston, I made a promise to you, and now I ask you to make a promise to me. Don't tell Rosaleen that I bought the brooch."

"I won't. You love her that much, don't you?" His soft tone sounded distant.

"Yes." Jacob watched the expression on the man's face closely, but Alistair gave little away. The wince could very well have been from the pain of his wound.

"She's in love with you, too, you know." An odd grin pulled up the corners of Ralston's lips. "In my line of work, you learn to read people. Listen"—a frown puckered his forehead—"beware of a gent by the name of McGurty. He'll have designs on Rosaleen."

"She told me about him." A sudden fear twisted inside Jacob. What if he were in Madison? "The man survived the sinking of the *Cortland Belle*?"

"Can't rightly say."

"You haven't seen him?"

Ralston shook his head. "No. Heard it both ways, but then—" Several more wracking coughs took him. "You can't take as gospel what fellers deep in their cups say over a blackjack table."

Jacob studied Ralston's face. The best he could discern, the man's answer seemed candid. "What does McGurty look like?" Madison teemed with strangers from the steamboats. A description of the man would be helpful.

The gambler's features took on a thoughtful look. " 'Bout your height. In his forties, I'd reckon. Black Irish. Black hair, thinnin' some and streaked with gray. Little black eyes, dead cold as polished onyx—stares right through a body. Chills ya to your soul. Got a bit of a paunch. Likes good food, drink, and women, not especially in that order." A wheezing cough that troubled Jacob interrupted Alistair's description of McGurty.

"Here, take a drink of water." Jacob filled a glass from the pitcher Rosaleen had left on the table by the bed.

"A real dandy dresser," Alistair continued after a sip of the water had eased his cough. "Always carries a silver-headed, ebony walking stick."

"Thanks." Jacob offered the man his hand and was surprised at the strength of his grip, even in his weakened state. "I'll fetch Dr. Morgan."

Later, Jacob placed the brooch in the cigar box where he'd kept his bell money. In a few days, Rosaleen would be leaving for New York. He'd like to think that Ralston's perception of her feelings about him were correct. Maybe they had been once. But he felt certain he'd destroyed any hope of rekindling her love.

His heart twisted as he gazed at the jeweled pin. Maybe when he presented it to her as a farewell present, she'd at least remember him with some measure of kindness.

nineteen

After Dr. Morgan treated Alistair Ralston, Rosaleen followed him and Jacob to the hallway outside Alistair's room.

Ephraim Morgan turned a stern look toward Rosaleen. "Jacob was right to fetch me, Rosaleen. I know you were trying to protect Mr. Ralston, but by not calling me sooner, you allowed your friend to become dangerously ill."

Rosaleen gave him a penitent nod. She sent up a prayer of thanks that God found a way to get the doctor here without her having to break her promise to Alistair.

The doctor's features relaxed to a reassuring smile. "He should heal fine as long as the fever doesn't return and the wound doesn't become infected again."

Brightening, Dr. Morgan turned his attention to Jacob. "Becky tells me Roscoe Stinnett has offered to put up the collateral in order to procure a loan for the church. That's great news."

"Yes, it is." Jacob fidgeted, seeming uninterested in elaborating on the subject.

An awkward moment of silence ensued while Rosaleen and Jacob watched the doctor descend the stairs.

Rosaleen broke the silence. "I'm glad you're going to get your church rebuilt, Jacob. That is wonderful." She meant it, too, but at the same time wondered if he'd taken Roscoe up on his offer concerning Sophie after all. If so, why had Jacob not told her? Was he too embarrassed to admit he'd made such a deal?

"Thank you." His gaze skittered away from hers.

She managed to push her trembling lips into a smile. "I'm glad you didn't listen to me and went in to see about Alistair."

"Me, too." He grinned. "He's not such a bad fellow for a

gambler and a rogue. He'll soon be off running his thimble-rig again with the best of them."

"I'd like to think I could convince him to reform, but I'm afraid it is unlikely, even with all my prayers."

"I'm sure you've planted the good seeds, Rosaleen. In the end, praying is the best thing we can do." His smile faded. "You'll be leaving with him, then?"

"No." Rosaleen's heart felt as wounded as Alistair's chest. If only she could have stayed. If only things had turned out differently. "Alistair will be going places I don't care to go now and doing things I know Jesus would not want me to be a party to."

"I'm glad to hear that. Then you'll be leaving on your own for New York?" His voice sounded strained. Did he want her to stay?

She fought the tears stinging behind her eyelids.

Please, Jacob, beg me to stay. Take me in your arms and tell me you want me to stay here with you forever.

She struggled to inject lightness into her answer. "Yes, I promised Alistair I'd take care of him until he's well. Then I'll begin my journey to New York."

The corner of Jacob's mouth lifted. "I'd very much like it if you'd continue to play for services while you remain in Madison. Would you do that for us and save the congregation a little while longer from Myrtle Stinnett's charity?"

Her heart galloped when he took her hands into his. Both their gazes focused on their clasped hands.

"Yes, Jacob, I'd like that very much." Hope withered. If he still loved her and hadn't given his promise to Sophie, now was the time he should beg her to stay—to entreat her never to leave him. Tears she couldn't allow him to see stung Rosaleen's eyes. Pulling her hands away from his strong, warm fingers, she fled down the stairs.

⁂

During the next couple of weeks, Rosaleen used the excuse of caring for Alistair to avoid Jacob. Though she'd relinquished the hope of ever becoming Jacob's wife, she held tight to her newfound faith. She'd always love Jacob. How could she not? He'd led her to the knowledge that God did indeed love her and would one day welcome her into heaven.

She longed to share this promise with others. Perhaps she could find a way to use her musical talents for the Lord. At present, she'd content herself with sharing the gospel with Alistair. Though an admitted challenge, he presented a captive audience.

"Never thought you'd become a church lady." Grinning, he shook his head, interrupting her daily scripture reading.

"I'm not a church lady. I'm a Christian." Rosaleen closed the Bible on her lap. "Alistair, you could have died. Aren't you concerned about what lies beyond?"

"Don't reckon I like to give it much thought." He grimaced, shifting to a more comfortable sitting position on the bed.

"Well, you need to think about it." She set the Bible on the table by the bed and bent over to adjust the pillows behind his head.

"You'll make a right pretty angel someday, Rosaleen." His gray gaze looked a little sad as he ran the back of his curled fingers across her cheek. Then his demeanor perked up with his voice. "I do like the music, though. I never knew you played the piano." He leaned his head back on the pillow and closed his eyes.

"I didn't before I went to the finishing school. I suppose I can thank my guardian for that, even if he did send me for selfish reasons. Funny how the Lord can take a bad situation and turn it into a blessing."

She'd been astounded at how much lighter her heart had become after she obeyed Christ's command and forgave Wilfred and Irene Maguire. With repeated reading, she'd etched into her heart Jesus' words from Matthew 5:44: *"But I say unto you, Love your enemies, bless them that curse you, do good to them that hate you, and pray for them which despitefully use you, and persecute you."*

Black Jack Bill McGurty? He'd be far harder to forgive, but Rosaleen would try.

Alistair rolled his head on the pillow, his gray eyes peering at her from beneath half-open lids. "Would you sing me that song again? The one about the rock."

Rosaleen smiled. Perhaps she could get through to Alistair with her music. She softly sang "Rock of Ages" until his deep, even breathing told her he'd fallen asleep.

A recurrence of infection along with another bout of fever had kept Alistair bedridden. But under the watchful care of Dr. Morgan, he was now showing steady improvement, causing the doctor to predict Alistair would be back on his feet within the week. Rosaleen would soon be free to leave for New York. A pang of sadness accompanied the thought as she slipped quietly from Alistair's room and climbed to her own room in the attic.

Knowing she would need to prepare for that day, Rosaleen stuck her hand into the mattress slit and felt for the calico sack. Finding it, she separated one of the ten-dollar notes from the fold of bills, shoved it into her apron pocket, and headed downstairs.

Exiting through the kitchen door, she paused on the path between the boardinghouse and the garden to glance back at the gray brick building. It hurt to think of leaving Madison and all the people who'd become dear to her. Yet if Jacob had wanted her to stay, he could have asked. Her heart still stung from the fact that he hadn't.

Squaring her shoulders, she raised her chin. She must concentrate on practicalities. She'd need a small steamer trunk or portmanteau to transport her few but precious possessions to New York. She could probably procure what she needed at King and Brother Merchants on Second Street.

"Rosaleen!" Patsey's cry sounded tight with pain.

Whirling toward the garden patch, Rosaleen caught sight of Patsy's red head kerchief, just visible above the browning leaves of the potato plants.

"I—I think the baby's comin'." Sitting in the dirt amid the drying vegetation, Patsey glanced down at her drenched calico skirt.

"But it's too soon! It's almost a month too soon." Rosaleen fought mounting fear.

"Reckon you'd best tell that to this young'un." Groaning, Patsey doubled over.

Rosaleen's mind raced with her heart. Andrew was down at the building site of the church with Jacob. She didn't know whether it would be better to help Patsey up or have her sit until she could get Andrew.

Oh God, just help me know what to do.

Drawing a deep breath, she forced her mind to rational thought. *Mrs. Buchanan will know what to do.*

"Just sit still, Patsey. I'll find Opal."

Patsey's answering groan warned there might not be a moment to spare.

Racing through the kitchen, Rosaleen began calling for Opal.

"Rosaleen, what on earth—" Opal began as she emerged from the dining room.

Interrupting, Rosaleen caught her hand. "Patsey's in the garden. I think she's in labor."

Opal paled and bolted for the kitchen door.

Rosaleen ran to catch up with the older woman's long-legged strides, directing her to the spot where she'd left Patsey.

"Come on, Patsey, you can't have this baby in the tater patch." Opal grasped Patsey under the arms and carefully but firmly lifted her straight up.

Together, Opal and Rosaleen helped Patsey into the house.

"I know it won't be easy, Patsey, but we must get you upstairs to a bed," Opal urged in a no-nonsense tone as she and Rosaleen practically carried Patsey between them.

"I can make it," Patsey gasped. "Ain't gonna' have this chil' on the floor or the dining room table, neither!"

Rosaleen breathed a relieved sigh when they reached the second floor.

They maneuvered the mother-to-be into a room Rosaleen had readied for prospective boarders. Opal yanked the covers down on the bed, sat Patsey on the edge of the mattress, and then turned to Rosaleen. "I'll get her into a nightdress. You hurry and fetch Andrew and Jacob."

Rosaleen flew down the stairs, out the boardinghouse, and up Mulberry Street. She raced down Main-Cross Street and just missed being hit by a passing carriage.

Oh God, give me strength and speed.

By the time she reached the church, her burning lungs felt as if they might burst.

"Rosaleen!" Jacob caught sight of her and threw his hammer to the ground with a thud. "What's happened?" Running to her, he drew her into his arms and held her while she gasped for breath to speak.

"It's Patsey." She gulped a lungful of air. "The baby's coming."

At his wife's name, Andrew dropped the wheelbarrow of bricks he'd been pushing, paying it no heed as it toppled and spilled its contents onto the ground. His dusky face blanched to only a few shades darker than Jacob's, and he raced for the wagon.

Her legs spent, Rosaleen sagged against Jacob. She allowed his tightened arm around her waist to propel her to the wagon. He helped her up then climbed to the seat beside her.

Andrew hollered and smacked the reins down hard against the mules' backs. The animals bolted, causing the wagon to lurch to a dizzying speed.

The wagon bed full of lumber bounced and clattered as they careened along. Rosaleen clung to Jacob, fearing they might overturn at the junction of Main-Cross and Mulberry. There, they narrowly missed a wagonload of pork barrels.

Ignoring the frightened neighs of the rearing horses and the angry protests of their driver, Andrew urged the mule team around the corner, stopping only when they reached Opal Buchanan's boardinghouse.

In a blur, Patsey's husband leaped from the wagon, bounded

to the porch, and shot through the front door.

Jacob helped Rosaleen down then climbed back to the wagon seat. "I'll go get Ephraim," he called over his shoulder as he turned the wagon around.

Rosaleen nodded and headed inside. Upstairs, she informed Opal and the expectant parents that Jacob had gone to fetch Dr. Morgan.

Andrew nodded but kept his eyes fastened on Patsey's face, scrunched with pain. Kneeling beside his wife's bed, he gently took her hand in his. In soothing tones, he whispered words of love and encouragement.

"First babies always take a while," Opal said lightly, bathing Patsey's face with a wet cloth. But the lines around the older woman's mouth looked tight.

When Dr. Morgan arrived with Jacob, the concern on his face struck fear in Rosaleen's heart. He immediately banished her and Jacob from the second story. He allowed Opal, and on Patsey's insistence, Andrew, to remain in the room.

Guilt-ridden, Rosaleen sank forlorn to the settee in the parlor. She'd spent too much time the past couple of weeks with Alistair, shifting a larger portion of the household work to Patsey. Now Patsey and her baby might have to pay with their lives. The thought was more than Rosaleen could bear. Slumping forward, she sobbed into her hands.

"Ephraim has delivered lots of babies. I'm sure everything will be fine," Jacob's quiet voice comforted.

"It's my fault," she choked through the sobs. "I spent too much time attending to Alistair and not helping Patsey."

His soft voice murmured consolation. "No, my dear Rosaleen. No." Sitting down beside her, he gathered her into his arms and rocked her against him. "You know Opal would never allow Patsey to do more than she should. You felt an obligation to Mr. Ralston. You are not to blame—not in any way."

Rosaleen wondered how she could have been so selfish. Why had she not once thought of Patsey's condition during the past two weeks? "If anything should happen to Patsey or the baby, I don't know if I could bear it." Devastated, she clung to Jacob, weeping against his neck.

"Shh, my sweet, don't do this to yourself. It is not your fault. Ephraim says many times babies come early and only God knows why." He pushed away enough to wipe the tears from her cheeks with his thumbs. "I think we should go to God right now, don't you?"

She nodded, reluctant to leave the haven of his embrace.

Holding her hands in his, he pressed the side of his face against hers. His breath felt soft, warm, and comforting against her ear as he whispered a prayer for Patsey and her baby's safety.

&

The sound of an infant's lusty cries caused them to spring apart. Jumping up, they ran to the bottom of the stairs.

After a few breathless moments, Dr. Morgan came to the second-story landing at the top of the stairway, his shirtsleeves rolled up to his elbows. "It's a boy," he announced, grinning. "He's a bit small, but by the sound of him, there's nothing wrong with his lungs. Patsey's exhausted but doing well," the doctor said before returning to Patsey's room.

"Thank You, Jesus!" Jacob shouted his prayer of thanks.

"Yes, Jesus, thank You! Thank You!" Rosaleen echoed, wiping the tears from her face. She felt weak as the tension drained away from her body.

Jacob and Rosaleen fell into each other's arms, their mutual relief gushing out in joyful laughter. When Rosaleen pushed away, Jacob gazed into her eyes. His smile faded as he whispered her name. Suddenly his eyes closed and his arms tightened around her, his mouth capturing hers.

Returning his caresses, Rosaleen floated for a glorious moment in the fantasy of her beautiful dream before reality gripped her. *No! I mustn't do this. Not until Jacob makes his intentions clear. Not until he asks me to stay.*

Shaken, she pulled away from him and fled upstairs.

After Dr. Morgan left, Rosaleen tidied up Patsey's room, glad to have something to take her mind off the kiss she'd shared with Jacob.

Opal washed the newborn infant then swaddled him in a soft cotton towel.

"He is the most beautiful thing I've ever seen," Rosaleen said, tensing as Opal placed the tiny, squirming infant in her arms. "I've never held a baby, let alone a newborn baby."

"You're doin' fine. Just support his head," Opal instructed with a smile.

"We've decided to call him Adam, since he's our first," Patsey said, grinning from her bed. "Andrew couldn't wait to git over to Georgetown to crow about him."

"I should think so, with a fine son like little Adam here." Rosaleen carefully deposited the mewling baby in the crook of his mother's arm.

Offering to start supper while Opal tended to the new mother and baby, Rosaleen descended the stairs. Jacob was nowhere in sight, and she was glad. Her heart still quaked from their impulsive kiss.

As she neared the bottom step, three quick raps sounded at the front door. She answered the door and blinked in surprise to find Sophie Schuler's beaming countenance.

"I'm afraid Jacob is not here," Rosaleen said, managing a weak smile.

"It's not Jacob I want to talk to. It's you."

"Me?" What business could Sophie have with her? The answer came as swiftly and unexpectedly as a stiletto through the heart.

"Oh, Rosaleen," she said with an excited squeal, "I so have the hypo, I can scarcely contain myself!"

Rosaleen knew from her time at the finishing school that "hypo" was a term young ladies used to express extreme excitement.

"I've just become engaged to be married, and I want you to play for my engagement party as well as for my wedding."

Staring at Sophie's face crinkling with excitement, Rosaleen felt the blood drain from her own. So Jacob had gone directly from kissing her to proposing marriage to Sophie.

twenty

On the front porch, Sophie bobbed back and forth, her hoop skirt swaying like a tolling bell. "Could I speak with you in the parlor, please?"

"Yes, of course. Please come in." Reeling from the shock of Sophie's announcement, Rosaleen tried to remember her manners. She stepped aside, allowing Sophie to swish past her into the front hallway. As she led the girl to the parlor, Rosaleen knew she must not forget that Sophie was an innocent in all this. "Would you like some tea, Miss Schuler?"

"No, please don't trouble yourself." Sophie carefully arranged her skirts as she lowered herself to the settee. "I am most anxious to discuss the particulars with you."

"Well, Miss Schuler"—Rosaleen hesitated as she took a seat opposite Sophie—"I'm not at all sure my participation will be possible." With sheer force of will, she battled the tempest raging inside her. It took all her strength to stay seated in the armchair, wearing what she hoped was a pleasant expression on her face. "Actually, I'm not planning to stay in Madison much longer."

In truth, Rosaleen longed to race to her room, grab her fifty dollars, and leave Madison with the clothes on her back by whatever means available.

"Oh." Sophie's delicate features wilted. "Edwin will be so disappointed."

"Edwin?" Rosaleen blinked in confusion.

"Yes, my fiancé, Edwin Applegate."

Astonishment, relief, and confusion swirled through Rosaleen. "You're—you're not marrying Jacob?"

"Jacob? Good heavens, no!" Sophie cackled. "I must confess I considered it once or twice when I was a child. But now that I'm grown, I find my affection for Jacob more closely resembles that for my brother, Will." As she exhaled a soulful sigh, a dreamy look came into her pale blue eyes, and she pressed her hand against her heart. "Only Edwin, my darling Edwin, causes my heart to take flight, then lighting, it indulges itself in hours of happy contemplation of our coming union."

Rosaleen couldn't help smiling at Sophie's poetic effusion, so representative of young ladies of the social elite.

"My engagement ball is only two weeks away. Surely you can stay that long." Her eyes hopeful, Sophie bit her bottom lip.

"Yes, I suppose I could." Still attempting to adjust to this new revelation, Rosaleen found the smile came much easier to her lips.

"Oh, that is wonderful!" Clapping her gloved hands together, Sophie actually bounced on the settee. "Of course, you must have a new gown for the occasion. I will send Aunt Myrtle's seamstress to take your measurements."

"I—I really can't afford a gown. . ." Every precious dollar Rosaleen had gotten for her brooch would be needed for her trip to New York, not to mention accommodations.

"Oh, fiddle-dee-dee!" With a flip of her hand, Sophie dismissed the concern. "Uncle Roscoe and Aunt Myrtle are paying for everything. The weather has stayed warm, so Swiss muslins and linen lawns would be permissible, but this being an evening affair, we simply must be in silks and taffetas. Don't you agree?"

"I—I suppose."

Sophie is not marrying Jacob. The thought drowned out the girl's prattle about the newest fabrics that had just arrived at the dry goods store.

Rosaleen mentally wrestled with the puzzling turn of events.

If Jacob isn't planning to marry Sophie, why hasn't he asked me to stay in Madison? He'd once asked her to marry him—begged her to marry him. He confessed that he'd wrongly accused her of gambling at the Billiard Saloon, even asking her forgiveness for his hasty judgment. Had he since thought better of it and decided to leave well enough alone after she'd called off their engagement?

"Rose. Yes, rose for Rosaleen," Sophie said with a giggle.

"What?"

"Rosaleen, you *must* keep up!" Sophie gave an exasperated sigh. "I said, with your coloring, that rose silk I saw at Fitch & Williams would be just perfect for you, don't you think?"

Rosaleen smiled. "That sounds wonderful. I can't wait to see it." There would be plenty of time to assimilate the heart-jarring news. Just now, Sophie deserved her full attention.

After a half hour of discussing quadrilles, ballads, and serenades, Sophie rose, smoothing wrinkles from her apricot lawn skirt. "Well, I have a million things to do and little time to accomplish them all."

Rosaleen hugged Sophie, realizing she hadn't even offered the girl her best wishes. "Please allow me to extend my most sincere felicitations."

"Thank you, Rosaleen." Sophie gave her a quick peck on the cheek. "I can scarcely wait to tell Edwin you've agreed to play for our engagement ball." Her eyes grew round while her little pink lips drew into a dainty pout, reminding Rosaleen of a child begging for a treat. "Won't you please consider staying until after the wedding in October? It would mean so much to us if you were to play for our wedding."

"I will consider it," Rosaleen said as she walked Sophie to the front door.

Returning to the parlor, Rosaleen stood at the front window and watched Sophie's carriage drive away. Her heart sagged with her shoulders. Jacob had said he wasn't in love with Sophie. Now she must assume, despite the kiss they'd shared earlier, he must have decided he wasn't in love with Rosaleen, either.

                    ❧

Jacob stood in the Madison Branch Bank beside Roscoe Stinnett. "I want to thank you for this loan, Roscoe," he said dipping a pen into an inkwell and scratching his signature onto the document. "I reiterate the fact that it is a *loan*. You will be paid back with interest."

"I'm a businessman, Reverend. Loans are part of what I do." Stinnett cleared his throat. "Besides, Myrtle and Sophie have their hearts set on that wedding taking place in your new church. If I don't make that happen, there'll be no living with them."

Their business concluded, they exited the bank together.

Jacob couldn't help a little grin. "Still, I thank you. The church will provide more room for a larger number of worshipers at services, and I pray many more souls won to Christ. You've done a good thing this day, Roscoe."

Roscoe only nodded, but Jacob noticed a softening of his hard-shelled, all-business facade. Never having had children of his own, the man seemed to have been blindsided by the wiles of his niece.

As Sophie had predicted, soon after her uncle allowed Edwin Applegate to court her, Roscoe grudgingly agreed to the match. Jacob hoped the young couple's relationship would help repair the rift between Roscoe and the elder Applegate.

With a handshake, the two men parted company.

Jacob touched his vest pocket where the copy of the loan crinkled beneath his fingers. He felt glad but not joyful. This was what he'd wanted for two years—plenty of money for material and labor to build the church. He was glad, too, that he'd be able to pay Andrew in a timely fashion for his masonry work on the church. With the arrival of baby Adam, Andrew and Patsey could well use the money. So why, Jacob wondered, wasn't he shouting his thanksgiving to the heavens?

What had dulled the joy in his heart?

"Rosaleen."

Her name floated from his lips on a soft sigh of regret. He hadn't realized how long he'd imagined standing before his congregation in the new church and seeing her lovely face beaming up at him from beside the piano. He swallowed hard, blinking quickly as Mulberry Street dimmed before him.

Two days ago, when Alistair Ralston left Madison, Jacob had breathed a sigh of relief to find that Rosaleen had indeed stayed behind at the boardinghouse. He'd thanked God when he learned that Sophie had managed to persuade Rosaleen to stay and play for her and Edwin's engagement party. He prayed that Sophie might convince her to play for the couple's wedding in October as well.

Entering the boardinghouse, Jacob reminded himself of Christ's promise: "And all things, whatsoever ye shall ask in prayer, believing, ye shall receive."

Believing. That was the thing. Did he truly believe he could win her love again, convince her to stay and be his wife? The larger question remained: *Do I even deserve her love?*

He felt a sardonic grin pull up his mouth at the absurd question. Of course he didn't deserve her love. He'd made a grand mess of everything. He'd wrongly accused her of gambling and impropriety and even questioned her conversion and honesty.

Jacob winced at the excruciating memory. How *could* she love him? How could she even think of marrying a man who'd accused her of such things?

"Did you get the loan?" Rosaleen asked, stepping from the dining room into the hallway.

"Yes." Jacob touched his chest where his heart raced beneath the folded document in his vest pocket. Lately, he found himself studying Rosaleen with a sense of urgency. Every curve of her face. The way the afternoon sun revealed glints of copper in her wavy, auburn hair. It seemed imperative that he commit each detail to memory.

"I'm glad." Her gaze dropped to the carpet when his lingered on her face.

"It's a blessing that Sophie was so adamant about getting married in the new church," he said in an attempt to prolong their conversation. The afternoon sun shafting down through the second-story window wreathed her in a golden glow. If he could keep her here at the foot of the stairs for a few moments longer, he might burn the image indelibly into his mind.

"This time I'm taking no chances." He reached into his pocket and pulled out the insurance papers he'd had drawn up. "Roscoe insisted that the church be insured." Rosaleen smiled and nodded, but the fact that she wouldn't meet his gaze hurt.

Jacob wished Mr. Blackmore down at the Delaware Mutual Insurance Company issued policies insuring against broken hearts.

Maybe if he could convince her to stay in Madison a little longer. . . "Sophie mentioned to me last Sunday how happy she is that you've agreed to play for her engagement ball. She confessed that she hopes to entice you to remain for the wedding." Jacob's hope faded when Rosaleen glanced away.

"I—I don't know. Sophie's wedding is set for mid-October, and I'd like to travel while the weather is still warm."

"On the whole, the weather should remain very clement through October." She'd loved him once. If she allowed him time to show her he was completely repentant, perhaps she could love him again. "Please consider it, Rosaleen. It would mean so much—to Sophie."

His heart nearly stopped when she raised her face. Her beautiful blue-green eyes glistened as her gaze seemed to search his. "If it means that much—to Sophie—then I will consider it. I will give her a definite answer at her engagement ball."

As he watched her ascend the stairs, Jacob's heart crawled to the mercy seat of his Lord. He, too, had been invited to Sophie and Edwin's engagement ball next week. Something he'd seen in Rosaleen's eyes rekindled within him a tiny spark of hope, and his heart refused to concede defeat.

I know I don't deserve her, Lord, but I may have one last chance—just one. Please guide me. Don't let me mess this one up as well.

twenty-one

Patsey tugged at the back of Rosaleen's silk gown. "If you don't stand still, I'll never get this buttoned up!"

Rosaleen stopped fidgeting and gazed out the second-story window down onto Mulberry Street. The view did little to calm her nerves. Through the deepening dusk, she could see the shiny black landau with its beaver-hatted driver waiting in front of the boardinghouse. The Stinnetts had sent the open carriage to transport her and Jacob to Sophie and Edwin's engagement party. Rosaleen tried to forget that in a few minutes she'd be riding through the summer evening opposite Jacob. "Are you sure you should be doing this? I could get Opal to help me."

An impatience-laden puff of breath sounded. "It's been two weeks since I had Adam, and if you and Mrs. Buchanan don't quit babyin' me, I'm gonna scream," Patsey said. "Now turn around and let's take a look at you."

Raising her face to the bureau mirror, Rosaleen had to admit she was pleased with the fabric Sophie had chosen for her. The rose silk gown showed off her hair and complexion to their greatest advantage.

Patsey tucked tiny rambling rose blossoms above the ringlets she'd fashioned at Rosaleen's temples. "Well, I don't know what Miss Schuler's gonna wear, but you're the woman every man'll be eyein' tonight."

"No one is going to pay much attention to the piano player, Patsey."

"'Cept Rev'rend Hale."

"Patsey!" Rosaleen strove to keep her voice light but saw her smile fade in the mirror.

Patsey slipped another pin into Rosaleen's hair to secure the blossoms. "Don't know what's come between you two, and it ain't none of my business, but I'm prayin' God'll use this evenin' to help mend it. All right," she said with a smile and a hug, "I'm done makin' you nervous."

Rosaleen adjusted the lace shawl over her bare shoulders, her heart quickening. She ignored Patsey's veiled attempt to garner information. As much as she'd love to unburden her heart to her friend, the wound still felt too raw to touch with words.

"Thanks, Patsey, I can use all of your prayers." Swallowing salty tears, Rosaleen gave Patsey a warm hug.

A sense of bereavement gripped Rosaleen at the thought of leaving her best friend behind when she left Madison. The only way she could stay would be if Jacob asked her to. Her hope of that happening diminished with each passing day. He'd had every opportunity to ask her again to marry him, yet he hadn't.

Rosaleen believed with all her heart that Jesus had wiped away her sins. Yet deep down, she wondered if Jacob could ever see her as pure. He'd once questioned her sincerity.

When he looks at me, does he still see a smudge on my soul? The thought pierced her when she met Jacob's formal countenance and rather stiff smile at the bottom of the stairs.

Other than his complimenting her appearance and their mutual agreement that it was, indeed, a fine evening, they accomplished the ride to the Stinnett home in virtual silence.

He looked as ill at ease as she felt. She thought his attitude seemed extra quiet, pensive even. Seeming to avoid her gaze, he fixed his attention on the passing scenery beyond the carriage.

Had he been disappointed that Sophie had chosen Edwin Applegate? Though curious about his thoughts at this moment, she wondered if God might have blessed her by sparing her the pain of that disclosure.

Resting against the black velvet upholstery of the carriage,

Rosaleen felt like a grand lady. Yet a sadness wrapped around her heart as the matched pair of dappled grays clopped along Mulberry Street, transporting them through the summer evening.

Glancing at her handsome companion caused an ache deep within her. How painful to be given a glimpse of what her life might have been like here in Madison with Jacob, yet to know it would never be.

They turned onto High Street, and she looked to her left. A block away, the red and gold August sunset spilled across the surface of the Ohio River, painting the water with its vivid hues.

What a hauntingly beautiful place.

Her heart clenched. She'd come to love the town almost as much as she loved the man sitting opposite her in the carriage. When she left, she'd be leaving a very large part of her heart in Madison, Indiana.

When they reached the front of the Stinnett house, the driver let down the steps of the carriage with a rattle. Jacob climbed from the carriage first then helped her down.

At the front door, a young housemaid with an Irish accent took her shawl and Jacob's white beaver hat. She ushered them into a large double parlor. There, a crystal chandelier tinkled above them with the movement of the milling guests. It cast a golden glow over the expanse of the bare wood floor, polished to a high gloss. The room had been emptied of all furniture except for some seating around the walls and the piano in the corner.

Rosaleen searched the room for familiar faces. Besides the Stinnetts, she recognized the Applegates and Dr. and Mrs. Morgan. Jacob's sister, clinging to the arm of her tall, handsome husband, looked stunning in a lilac taffeta gown.

Sophie's azure silk skirt whispered as she fairly skipped toward them, a tall, bespectacled young man in tow. "Oh Rosaleen," she squealed, "you look lovely! I just knew that color would be perfect for you."

"Thank you again for the dress—"

"Oh, fiddle-dee-dee!" Sophie swept aside her expression of gratitude with a giggle and a shake of her blond curls. "I don't believe you've been formally introduced to my fiancé, Edwin Applegate." She lifted an adoring smile to the shy visage of the young man beside her.

"Mr. Applegate, I do remember seeing you with your sister at worship services," Rosaleen said, offering him her hand.

"Mrs. Archer," Edwin murmured, dipping a quick nod of his reddish-blond head over her hand. He brushed his lips across the top of her fingers, and then his chocolate-brown gaze drifted back to his diminutive fiancée.

Sophie grinned at Jacob. "Everything is perfect. Edith is prepared, just as planned."

Before Rosaleen could ponder the girl's cryptic comment to Jacob, Sophie whisked her toward the piano with instructions concerning the order in which the tunes were to be played.

"I hope this evening will be as wonderful for you as it is for me." Sophie gave her a quick squeeze then skipped away to join Edwin and Jacob.

Unable to guess what Sophie had meant by her statement, Rosaleen dismissed it as a manifestation of the girl simply being "hypo" about her engagement ball.

She'd played only two quadrilles when Jacob appeared beside the piano with Edwin's sister, Edith.

"I'd like very much to speak with you."

The seriousness of his expression both puzzled and troubled Rosaleen.

"I—I need to begin the serenades. Sophie expects—"

"Edith will take over." He clasped Rosaleen's hand in his, urging her up.

Edwin's twin sister settled herself in front of the piano, her sage green silk skirt rustling as she arranged it around the stool.

"Are you sure?" Rosaleen asked, bewildered as he led her across the parlor. She glanced back at the piano where Edith had begun playing the serenade "Come, the Moon Plays on the Roses." She didn't like thinking she was shirking her duty.

"I'm sure." He slipped his arm around her waist, guiding her toward the French doors that opened to the back veranda.

The boughs of the giant ash tree swayed in the gentle evening breeze, caressing the veranda with soft shadows. The fragrance of honeysuckle and roses hung heavily on the night air. "Rosaleen," he whispered her name as he took her hands into his.

Rosaleen's hammering heart glowed like the pale moonbeams shimmering across the dusky ribbon of the Ohio River.

His lips lifted in that familiar quirk of a smile so dear to her. "As lovely as that gown is, it lacks something." He reached into his vest pocket.

Flabbergasted, she gazed with widening eyes at the object in his open palm. "My brooch!" she blurted. "But I thought Alistair—"

"I bought it from him."

"But how?" Her mind spun. Alistair had wanted that brooch for a long time. He wouldn't have sold it cheaply. Had Jacob taken out a separate loan with Mr. Stinnett?

Suddenly, Rosaleen remembered Jacob's savings, and she emitted a soft gasp. His face blurred through her tears. "Oh, Jacob, no—not your bell money."

"This means more to me. You mean more to me than any bell, any building, anything else on the face of this earth."

Accepting the brooch, she stared at him mutely then caught her breath as he slowly sank to one knee before her.

"I know I don't deserve you." He lifted his tear-streaked face to hers. "I'm a wretched, sinful man, who has no right to ask for the love of a heart as pure as yours. Yet I do—I must.

I cannot bear to contemplate a life devoid of your presence. I pray you can find it in your sweet heart to forgive my grievous trespasses against you."

His blue eyes brimmed with remorse, and his voice palpitated with agony. "Nor do I have the right to ask you to give up your dream of traveling to New York. But if you can love me even a little, please say you'll stay in Madison and be my wife."

Rosaleen's heart pulsed with joy. Now she understood Sophie's peculiar comments. She must have been aware of Jacob's plans. Happy tears slid down her cheeks.

Oh, thank You, God! Thank You for answering Patsey's prayers. Prayers she realized she'd been too afraid to pray for herself. *Oh God, You are so wonderfully good, so loving and merciful.*

"I shall kneel here before you in petition until you give me an answer one way or another, or until Roscoe Stinnett throws me off his veranda."

Rosaleen felt a little laugh shake through a happy sob. Stunned by the unexpected events, she realized she'd left her darling still on his knees, his question unanswered. "Yes, oh yes, Jacob. I've never stopped loving you. Never."

Rising, he pulled her into his arms, smothering her tear-drenched words with his kisses.

The ball passed in a blurred whirl for Rosaleen. Jacob followed Sophie and Edwin's engagement announcement with his and Rosaleen's.

He kept Rosaleen from the piano for the remainder of the evening. They danced to quadrilles and serenades between congratulatory handshakes, hugs, and kisses by all present. To Rosaleen's amazement, even Roscoe Stinnett wished her well and offered her a kiss on the cheek and a belated welcome to Madison.

"Rosaleen, I'm so thrilled to be getting you for a sister." Becky Morgan gave her an excited hug. "We must make a date to go shopping for material for your wedding dress. Jacob is determined that your wedding be the first in the new church, so time is short."

Even as her heart soared on the winds of her beautiful dream come true, Rosaleen beat back an intangible fear. No, this time her future was secure. No evil could snatch it away.

&

It had been the better part of a week since the engagement ball, and Rosaleen still felt as if her feet had not touched ground.

Roscoe Stinnett hired a crew of carpenters to complete the church. However, Jacob, insisting that everything be perfect for their special day, spent every spare moment at the church, adding finishing touches of his own.

They'd agreed to a wedding date three weeks away. Rosaleen, also feeling the pressure of limited time, was thankful for Becky Morgan's offer of help.

In the boardinghouse's front hallway, Rosaleen hesitated at the front door. "Are you sure it's all right for me to leave this morning, Opal?" Feeling a little guilty, Rosaleen tied the ribbons of her gray silk bonnet beneath her chin. "I hate to leave you shorthanded on washday with two new boarders."

Opal snorted. "The day Patsey and I can't handle a washing and two salesmen is the day I shut down the boardinghouse! You run along now and let Mrs. Morgan help you pick out something special for your wedding dress."

As she neared the Fitch & Williams dry goods store, Rosaleen fingered her brooch pinned at the bodice of the green-sprigged muslin frock. Remembering Jacob's sacrifice, she felt warmth suffuse her heart. She smiled. Thanks to Edwin Applegate's persuasion, his father had offered to buy the bell for the church. It was just one more blessing in a bountiful harvest of God's blessings.

She gazed down Main-Cross Street. Becky Morgan had said she would need to get a widowed neighbor lady to sit with the children and might be a few minutes late.

"Well, well, it seems I've found you at last."

Rosaleen's heart lurched at the quiet voice behind her. An icy chill shot through her, and she whirled to face her nightmare.

twenty-two

Willing her voice to steadiness, Rosaleen tried not to focus on Bill McGurty's beady black eyes. "This is my home now. I'm never going back to the riverboats."

"Is that so?" His slow grin looked terrifyingly self-assured. "Well, we'll see about that."

She shivered as he tapped the silver tip of his ever-present ebony cane on the boardwalk. Many times she'd felt the sting of it against her flesh.

Hitching up her courage, she realized he could not hurt her here. He wouldn't dare try to abduct her in broad daylight on Main-Cross Street. "Yes, that is so. I'm engaged to be married and will be staying here in Madison."

"I heard." The quiet, congenial tone of his voice made it all the more frightening. "A young reverend, I understand." The sarcastic snort that followed this disclosure infuriated her. "My, my! What would he think if he knew—"

"Jacob knows everything!" *Oh Jesus, help me. Give me courage.* Rosaleen raised her chin in defiance. "You cannot intimidate me or drag me back to the riverboats!"

At his laughter, fear and anger mingled within her.

"My dear Rosaleen, who said anything about dragging you back? No, no, my dear"—he reached out and with a crooked finger, caught a strand of her hair that had escaped her bonnet—"I'm sure I can persuade you to come of your own accord."

Instinctively, she turned her head away and shrank from his touch. But then, swinging back to face him squarely, she glared at his confident smirk. Shaking with fury, she nearly spat her reply. "Nothing you could say or do would ever convince me to leave Jacob!"

"Jacob? Oh, you mean that nice-looking, blond young man I saw working alone on that church building on the corner of Broadway and Second Streets?"

"How do you know that?" she asked in a raspy whisper, panic robbing her of breath.

"Ask the right questions, and folk are always eager to help." His demeanor switched to a far more malicious posture. "It would be a real shame if anything bad were to happen to that young man," he said with a sneer. "I've looked too long and hard to simply turn on my heel and go back to the *James Seymour* without you!" His manicured fingers bit into her wrist. "Without a groom, you'll not be a bride. I killed your first husband in order to have you. Don't think for a second I wouldn't do it again and not twitch an eyelid!"

A sick feeling settled in the pit of her stomach at his revelation. She'd had no idea Bill had planned to kill Donovan before he ever sat down at that gambling table.

The sun glinted off the silver pocket watch he pulled from his scarlet brocade vest. "The *James Seymour* leaves Madison at five o'clock this evening. Be in front of the Madison Hotel in a half hour's time, or Jacob Hale will meet the same fate as Donovan Archer."

She didn't doubt it for an instant. In dismay, she heard the defeat-laden words drop from her lips. "I'll be there."

All thoughts of Becky Morgan and their morning of shopping were swept away in a tempest of mind-numbing terror.

Rosaleen hurried down Mulberry Street toward the boarding-house, cold fingers of fear tingling down her spine. Alarm consumed her. Bill knew exactly where Jacob was, and that he was alone.

Her mind raced. Patsey had said Andrew would be working on a masonry job near Hanover for the next several days. Even if she could get word to him, she'd only be putting him in danger as well. If she attempted to alert the sheriff, Bill might very well see her, kill Jacob, and slip away onto any number of steamboats or ferries leaving the Madison shore.

No. Jacob's only hope was for her to obey Bill.

Nearing the boardinghouse, she prayed she could get what she needed and leave without being noticed. She glanced behind the garden where newly washed sheets flapped and billowed in the breeze. The sound of Opal and Patsey's laughing chatter gave her a measure of hope.

She entered the front as quietly as possible, grimacing when the front doorbell emitted a tiny jingle. Hiking her skirt to her knees, she took the stairs two steps at a time.

Panting, she stumbled into her little attic room. Her hands shook as she rolled up the few frocks she owned and stuffed them into the leather portmanteau she'd bought at King and Brothers before the engagement ball. Reaching into the mattress, she grasped the remainder of her money and tucked it into the folds of her rose ball gown. She picked up the little Bible Jacob had given her and pressed it for a second to her heart before dropping it into the portmanteau.

Leaving, Rosaleen paused at the doorway, allowing her gaze to sweep the little room that had been her haven for the better part of four months. Bereft, she quietly closed the door and headed downstairs.

In the parlor, she went to Jacob's desk and took a sheet of paper from the stack he used to pen his sermons. Drawing a deep, ragged breath, she dipped the quill into the inkwell and forced her trembling hand to stillness.

Oh God, forgive me for the lie and let him believe this. Please, just let him believe this.

The scribbled words of her good-bye note blurred, and she sniffed back tears. She started to sign it "Love, Rosaleen," then scratched out the word "Love," and simply signed it "Rosaleen."

Out on Mulberry Street, she turned for one last, fond look at the boardinghouse. *Oh God, just let me get away unseen, and please, please protect Jacob!*

Numb, she clutched the portmanteau and hurried up

Mulberry, praying she could reach the Madison Hotel without running into Becky Morgan.

She fought to push from her mind images of what awaited her. There'd be plenty of time later to deal with the grief of her loss and the terror of Bill McGurty. Keeping Jacob safe was all that mattered now.

❧

The bottom of the oilcan popped beneath Jacob's thumb as he lubricated the last of the church doors' hinges. Assuring himself that the two oak doors worked perfectly, he opened and shut them several times.

He descended the four stone steps. His heart skipped with his feet as his hand slid along the wrought-iron railing. A few paces from the building, he turned to gaze at his dream, now a reality.

The redbrick church stood like a stalwart sentry looking down on the Ohio. The gleaming white cross atop the belfry would be visible to those passing on the river as well as from the Kentucky side. Thanks to the Applegates' generous hundred-dollar donation, the five-hundred-pound bell should be arriving next week from Cincinnati's Verdin Bell Company.

"Well, there it is, Orville." He glanced down at his friend's gravestone. "I hope it is everything you dreamed of."

A stiff river breeze brushed the gold-tinged willow branches against the headstone as if in nodding agreement.

"With God's help, I will work tirelessly to fill it, Orville. I promise." The smile spreading over his face reached all the way to the center of his heart. "I won't be alone in my work. I will soon have a wife to help me. I only wish you could have been here for my wedding." A sweet sadness tempered his joy. "You'd have loved Rosaleen," he whispered. "Her heart is as beautiful as her face, and she loves the Lord." He grinned down at Orville's marker. "The true miracle is that she says she loves me, too."

Walking down Mulberry Street, Jacob could not stop

smiling. He knew Rosaleen had planned a day of shopping with Becky. His pace quickened, eager to learn of her day and share with her all he'd accomplished at the church.

When he entered the boardinghouse parlor, the look of sadness on Opal Buchanan's face wiped the smile off his.

"Opal, what is it?" Fear tightened around his chest like an iron band. Had something happened to baby Adam, Andrew, or Patsey? Just then, he heard the baby's normal cry. Through the parlor doorway, he caught a glimpse of Patsey carrying Adam. Whispering soothing hushes, she headed upstairs with the infant.

"Oh Jacob, I'm so sorry." Opal held out a page of his letter paper that trembled in her hand.

"Rosaleen? Has something happened to Rosaleen?" Frantic, he rushed to the woman's side and snatched the paper from her hand, terror twisting his insides.

"I didn't want you to find it alone." Opal sank limply to the sofa.

Jacob had to read the terse missive three times over before his mind would assimilate its meaning. At last, he dropped numbly to the settee. Yet he could not budge his gaze from the unbelievable words that continued to rip at his shredded heart.

Jacob,
   I've come to realize that I cannot marry you after all but must follow my dream and journey on to New York. Please forgive me, and do not try to find me.

                                                   Rosaleen

His voice cracking, he raised his face to Opal's tear-streaked one. "Did she say anything to you—tell you why?"

"No, not a hint." Opal's befuddled voice shook. "She left this morning to go shopping with your sister, and I never saw her again. Patsey and I spent the entire morning behind the garden doing the laundry. When Rosaleen didn't return by noon, I began to wonder but figured they'd gone on to Becky's house."

"Becky must know something." With unsteady fingers, he folded the note and tucked it inside his shirt next to his heart. Though these few words had shattered his life, they were all he had left of Rosaleen. So in that, they were precious.

In a daze, he walked the distance from the boardinghouse to Becky's home.

Could everything have been an act? The thought was indescribably excruciating. His mind would not accept it. His heart would not accept it. *God help me. Show me what to do. She wouldn't have done this. Something is wrong! Something is terribly wrong!*

He pounded at his sister's front door with both fists.

The door eased open, revealing his sister's perturbed face. "Jacob, please! You don't have to knock down the door. Lucy is sleeping."

"What happened with you and Rosaleen today?" Ignoring Becky's admonishment, he strode past her into the front hall.

"Nothing." His sister's face held a bewildered blankness. "She never showed up. I was late arriving at Fitch & Williams. Mrs. Pearson wasn't feeling well and couldn't watch Daniel and Lucy, so I had to take them with me."

"She's gone." Somehow he managed to squeeze the painful words from his throat.

"You can't mean *gone.* Surely there's been a misunderstanding."

"Does this look like a misunderstanding?" He pulled Rosaleen's note from his shirt and handed it to his sister.

"Oh, Jacob, I can't believe she'd do this." Becky raised a baffled gaze from the paper in her hand. "She seemed so exited about your wedding—about staying here."

"I don't think she wanted to go." Daniel's small voice intruded from the bottom of the stairway.

Jacob and Becky turned to the boy, who stood looking down at his dusty shoes.

Rushing to his nephew, Jacob grasped the boy's shoulders.

"Daniel, what do you mean? Did you see Rosaleen today?" He tried to calm his racing heart. The child might only want attention. It could mean nothing. It could mean everything.

"I—I. . ." Daniel stammered, his dark eyes large with fear.

"Daniel!" Jacob nearly shouted in frustration.

"Jacob, you're scaring him." Becky's quiet voice and hand on his arm flooded Jacob with remorse.

"I'm sorry, Daniel." Kneeling beside his nephew, Jacob brushed the tears from the child's face. "Please, Daniel, I need to find Rosaleen. If you know anything, please tell me. Have you seen her today?"

Daniel nodded.

"Where?" It took all Jacob's strength to keep his voice calm.

"In front of the Madison Hotel," Daniel mumbled, dropping his gaze to his shoes again. "I saw her when me and Nate Ross went to the confectionary down by the carriage company."

"Daniel, it's 'Nate and I,'" Becky corrected her son's grammar, "and you know your father and I don't want you near that hotel alone!"

Ignoring his sister, Jacob turned back to his nephew, hope and fear tangling together inside him. "What did you mean when you said you didn't think she wanted to go?"

"An angry-looking man pushed her into a carriage, and she was crying."

"You're sure it was Rosaleen?"

"Yes. She was wearing that green and white dress that used to be Mama's."

In spite of his anxiety, Jacob felt a grin tug at his lips. It faded quickly. "Was it a tall man? A man as tall as your Papa, with reddish hair?" Could Alistair have returned after all and forced Rosaleen to go with him?

"No." Daniel shook his head. "He was kind of fat around his belly like Mr. Stinnett, but shorter. He had a black walking stick with silver at both ends."

Alistair Ralston's description of Bill McGurty slammed

to the front of Jacob's mind, filling him with fury and terror. *Always carries a silver-headed, ebony walking stick.*

"McGurty. Which way did the carriage go?"

"Down toward the river."

"Who's McGurty?" Becky asked.

"The man Rosaleen was running from when the *Cortland Belle* caught fire—the man who killed her husband."

Becky's hand flew to her mouth, stifling a gasp.

Jacob felt a rage he'd never known. *How dare he?* How dare the man come to Madison and pluck Rosaleen from his life? Had he been lying in wait at the hotel? Had McGurty threatened her? Jacob's mind spun with unanswered questions. Disappointment pierced his heart at the realization that Rosaleen hadn't trusted him to protect her from McGurty. Surely she knew he'd lay down his life for her without a second thought.

"Am I in trouble?"

Jacob felt his heart melt at Daniel's shaky question. "No, Daniel." He brushed the boy's dark hair from his face and placed a heartfelt kiss on his little nephew's head. "You may have just saved Rosaleen's life. I pray you have."

"Jacob, you can't go down to the riverfront alone. You don't know what that man might do." Becky gripped his arm, fear shining in her blue eyes. "Please wait until Ephraim returns from his call and can go with you."

"Becky, I can't wait. I can't risk that man's leaving Madison with Rosaleen. When Ephraim returns, have him fetch Sheriff Rea down to the docks." He forced a smile and gave his sister a quick hug and kiss on the cheek. "Just pray for us, Becky, and try not to worry."

Racing down Main-Cross Street, Jacob prayed with all his heart that he might rescue Rosaleen safely. But if his last act on earth before facing his Lord was an attempt to wrench her from McGurty's grasp, then so be it.

twenty-three

Breathing hard, Jacob stopped at the junction of Mulberry and Ohio Streets. He darted desperate glances up and down the docks. He'd run the full distance from his sister's home on Main-Cross then down Broadway past the church. But here at the riverfront, he paused, unsure which way to go.

It was Monday afternoon, so the steam packet *Wm. R. McKee* had left for Cincinnati hours ago, and the *Swiftsure* wouldn't be docking again until tomorrow morning. Several flatboats were loading barrels of pork from the numerous pork-packing plants, but he saw no signs of a ferry.

Suddenly, the blast of a steamboat whistle drew his attention several blocks east where East and Ohio Streets intersected. He raced to where the steamboat was docked. There, ladies in full skirts of satins and lawns, shaded by parasols, made a moving ribbon of color on the arms of broadcloth-clad, beaver-hatted gentlemen.

Battling panic, Jacob scanned the passengers embarking and disembarking the sternwheeler *James Seymour*. Out of the corner of his eye, he caught a glimpse of green and white on the top deck near the stern. Fear quickly swamped his initial feeling of relief.

"Rosaleen! Rosaleen!" The bustle of the busy riverfront drowned his calls. She would never hear him from this distance amid the off-loading of freight and the happy, loud chatter of passengers.

His heart leaped at the sight of her. She stood bareheaded, grasping the rail. Her light-colored frock stood out in stark contrast against the green and gold wooded hills of Kentucky behind her. Even at this distance, he could see the sun revealing coppery lights in her hair as the river breezes played with curling wisps of her dark auburn tresses.

Watching her turn and gaze upriver toward the church, he could only wonder what might be going through her mind and heart. He blinked away tears, remembering that morning last April when his heart first stirred at her beauty. The memory solidified his determination.

I won't let him have her. I won't!

Ignoring the protests of embarking passengers, Jacob elbowed his way up the boat ramp. She seemed to be alone. Perhaps if McGurty were otherwise occupied, Jacob just might be able to convince her to leave with him.

Oh God, just help me convince her to leave this boat!

ᴥ

The white cross atop the belfry of Jacob's church blurred. Rosaleen closed her damp eyes, and the image of her beloved's face appeared behind her eyelids. It seemed so real she might reach out and touch the scar on Jacob's cheek. She opened her eyes, unable to bear the agony of the vision any longer. She drew in a lungful of fresh air then exhaled a ragged breath, hoping Bill would not learn she'd disobeyed him.

Upon embarking, he'd shoved her into the tiny cabin with orders that she stay there until he finished a card game. Unwilling to leave Madison without another look, she'd dared to make her way to the outside deck. For a better look at the town, she'd climbed the stairs to the top deck. She'd deal with Bill and the consequences of her actions later. In truth, any punishment Bill might mete out paled in comparison to his having ripped her from the man she loved and the only place that had ever felt like home.

Gripping the railing, she fought the panic that urged her to flee this steamboat and run back to Opal's boardinghouse and into Jacob's sweet embrace. Yet to do so would be to seal her darling's fate. She had no doubt that Bill meant every word of his threat.

Dear Lord, help me. Give me the courage to save Jacob and leave it all behind.

From the top deck of the *James Seymour*, her gaze drifted along the shoreline of Madison, Indiana, and she stifled a sob. The place had entangled itself in her heartstrings. Dear faces she might never again see in this life swam before her eyes through a mist of tears. Yet one visage overshadowed them all, saturating her whole heart.

"Jacob." His name snagged on the ragged edges of her sobs.

"I'm here, my darling."

Catching her breath, she swung around, sure she'd imagined his voice. Unbelievably, his blond head emerged from the stairwell connecting the upper and middle decks.

Her heart seized as joy, love, and fear collided. She stepped toward him then felt her body jerk back as fingers bit into her arm.

"I told you to stay below. Now see what you've done? You've complicated things and put this nice young man in jeopardy." Bill McGurty's warm, whiskey-laced breath sent shivers through her.

"Let her go, McGurty." Jacob's voice was calm as he took a step toward them.

"Ah, I see my reputation precedes me." Bill slipped his left arm around her waist, holding her against him in a vice-tight grip. With his free hand, he pulled a walnut-handled derringer from his vest. Flicking his wrist, he motioned toward the stairwell with the little pistol. "Young reverend, I suggest you turn around and go back down those steps and off this boat if you want to preach another sermon."

Fear twisted through Rosaleen when Jacob continued to advance. "Go away, Jacob! Go back to the boardinghouse. I don't love you." *God, please let him believe it.*

A sweet smile lifted the corners of Jacob's mouth, and her hopes plummeted. "You're a terrible liar, Rosaleen."

"I suggest you listen to the little lady, Reverend." A tiny *click* told Rosaleen Bill had pulled the hammer back on the derringer.

"Not without Rosaleen," Jacob replied, his voice steady, his blue eyes as calm as the placid Ohio on a windless day.

To Rosaleen's horror, she saw him take another step toward her. The awful scenes of Donovan's death played before her eyes. She couldn't let that happen to Jacob. She wouldn't!

Please, God, give me the strength and courage to do this.

The words of one of the scriptures she'd committed to memory flashed to her mind: "*I can do all things through Christ which strengtheneth me.*"

The next few seconds passed as if in a nightmare. She leaned back and as far away from Bill as his grasp allowed. The low railing edging the steamboat's top deck bit into her lower back. With all her strength, she brought her arm closest to Bill forward then reared back, sinking her elbow into his ribs.

"Uhh!" His exclamation seemed more of surprise than pain, yet it caused him to double over and lower his hand that held the derringer. The shot pinged harmlessly into the deck.

The instant Bill's grip loosened, Rosaleen pulled free of him. Clinging to the rail, she watched, terrified, as Jacob plowed into Bill. The impact brought both men down and sent the spent, one-shot derringer clanging to the deck.

Rosaleen was relieved when Jacob managed to extricate himself from Bill's grasp and push up into a kneeling position. But when he glanced to his side as if looking for Rosaleen, Bill, who'd also righted himself, reached over and snatched his walking stick from the deck and swung it in an arc toward Jacob's head. The stick made contact with an ugly *smack*. A scream caught in Rosaleen's throat when another blow landed solidly against Jacob's jaw, sending him sprawling.

Bill scrambled to his feet and lunged at Rosaleen. "Come here, you little—" He slipped on the derringer, cutting his sentence short.

In shock, Rosaleen watched his feet go out from under him, the momentum of his lunge propelling his body over the short railing. For a moment, she sat motionless, stunned by what had just transpired.

Then her gaze fell upon Jacob, who'd righted himself and was rubbing his jaw. "Jacob, are you all right?" Weeping, she rushed to throw her arms around him.

"I thought I'd come to save *you*," he told her with a grin, holding her tight against him.

Two deafening blasts of the steamboat's whistle and the *shug, shug, shug* of the paddlewheel announced the *James Seymour*'s departure.

"Help me up, man! In the name of all that's holy."

In disbelief, Rosaleen's face swung with Jacob's toward the sound of Bill's voice. Somehow, he'd miraculously caught hold of the railing with one hand, saving himself from the deadly drop.

Pressing a quick kiss on her cheek, Jacob extricated himself from her embrace and went to assist his nemesis.

He almost had Bill up, when in horror, Rosaleen saw the sun glint on the barrel of a second derringer in McGurty's free hand. Jacob must have seen it at the last moment and jerked back, letting go of Bill's arm.

The instant the bullet whizzed past Jacob's ear, Bill fell backward to the churning water below. His head hit the iron rim of the giant paddlewheel with a sickening *crack*! An instant later, his body disappeared beneath the surface of the Ohio.

Trembling, Rosaleen stared down at the water.

"Don't look, darling. Don't look." Jacob pulled her away from the railing, stifling her sobs against his chest. Rocking her in his arms, he murmured sweet hushes while he kissed her hair.

Dimly aware of excited voices and a flurry of activity around them, Rosaleen noticed that the *James Seymour* had reversed, returning to the Madison shore. "Thank You, Jesus. Thank You, thank You." A bevy of thankful prayers winged their way heavenward from her grateful heart as she clung to Jacob, burying her face in his chest. Then a flash of quick anger blazed inside her and she pulled away from him. "Jacob,

I told you not to follow me. You could have been killed!"

"But I wasn't." He gave her that crooked grin of his that had won her heart her first day in Madison. "Hebrews 13:6 says, 'The Lord is my helper, and I will not fear what man shall do unto me.' Rosaleen, I was not going to let that man take you away from me."

She felt sure he knew, yet she couldn't let it go. She had to say it. "Jacob, when I told you I didn't love you, I didn't mean it. I do love you. I love you so much. I will love you every day for the rest of my life."

"I know, my darling." His beautiful blue gaze melted into hers. Smiling, he brushed the tears from her cheeks with his calloused thumb. "And I'll love you as long as God gives me breath." With his whispered confession, he pulled her into his arms and pressed his lips tenderly against hers.

epilogue

Boang! Boang! Boang!

The sound of the new church bell rang out, announcing to the town of Madison that God had just joined together the hearts and lives of two of His own.

Rosaleen Hale clung tightly to her husband's arm as they descended the stone steps of the church that had been his dream. Careful to hold the voluminous folds of her yellow silk skirt away from her feet, she scarcely noticed the congregation behind them calling out a potpourri of congratulations and good wishes.

Over her shoulder, she sent the crowd a smile and a wave before turning her gaze toward the Ohio River framed by the boughs of trees dressed in the deep reds, oranges, and golds of autumn. The undiluted joy in Rosaleen's heart matched the pristine clarity of the cloudless October sky.

"Happy, darling?" Jacob asked as he settled her on the maroon velvet seat of the phaeton.

Her husband's quiet question caressed her heart. "Superbly," she managed before a knot of emotion gathering in her throat rendered her mute. How could she articulate to her dear husband her wonder over all God had wrought in her life these past six months? Changes she'd never have imagined the night she fled the burning deck of the *Cortland Belle*.

Jacob flicked the reins against the sorrel mare's back, and they rolled down Broadway toward Ohio Street and the river.

Rosaleen gazed at the broad waterway that held so many memories, both sweet and awful. She marveled at how God had turned grief to joy, tragedy to triumph, and despair to hope. Since her father's death, she had ached to belong to a real family. Breathing a soft sigh of contentment, she snuggled in the circle of Jacob's arm. Now, thanks to her darling "angel," she belonged to the family of God and could look forward to a sweet life, as well as a sweet forever.

A Letter To Our Readers

Dear Reader:

In order that we might better contribute to your reading enjoyment, we would appreciate your taking a few minutes to respond to the following questions. We welcome your comments and read each form and letter we receive. When completed, please return to the following:

Fiction Editor
Heartsong Presents
PO Box 719
Uhrichsville, Ohio 44683

1. Did you enjoy reading *Sweet Forever* by Ramona K. Cecil?
   ❑ Very much! I would like to see more books by this author!
   ❑ Moderately. I would have enjoyed it more if

   _____

   _____

   _____

2. Are you a member of **Heartsong Presents**? ❑ Yes ❑ No
   If no, where did you purchase this book? _____

   _____

3. How would you rate, on a scale from 1 (poor) to 5 (superior), the cover design? _____

4. On a scale from 1 (poor) to 10 (superior), please rate the following elements.

   ____ Heroine   ____ Plot
   ____ Hero   ____ Inspirational theme
   ____ Setting   ____ Secondary characters

5. These characters were special because? _____

_____

_____

6. How has this book inspired your life? _____

_____

_____

7. What settings would you like to see covered in future
   Heartsong Presents books? _____

_____

_____

8. What are some inspirational themes you would like to see
   treated in future books? _____

_____

_____

9. Would you be interested in reading other **Heartsong
   Presents** titles? ❏ Yes ❏ No

10. Please check your age range:
   ❏ Under 18   ❏ 18-24
   ❏ 25-34   ❏ 35-45
   ❏ 46-55   ❏ Over 55

Name _____

Occupation _____

Address _____

City, State, Zip_____

VIRGINIA BRIDES

3 stories in 1

Traverse through Shenandoah Valley history. . .and love. When love starts to grow, will life's complications be too much to overcome? Can God bring good out of lives that seem to be spinning out of control?

Historical, paperback, 352 pages, 5³/₁₆" x 8"

Hearts♥ng

Any 12
Heartsong
Presents titles
for only
$27.00*

HISTORICAL ROMANCE IS CHEAPER BY THE DOZEN!
Buy any assortment of twelve *Heartsong Presents* titles and save 25% off of the already discounted price of $2.97 each!

*plus $3.00 shipping and handling per order and sales tax where applicable.
If outside the U.S. please call
740-922-7280 for shipping charges.

HEARTSONG PRESENTS TITLES AVAILABLE NOW:

___HP539 *Two Hearts Wait*, F. Chrisman
___HP540 *Double Exposure*, S. Laity
___HP543 *Cora*, M. Colvin
___HP544 *A Light Among Shadows*, T. H. Murray
___HP547 *Maryelle*, L. Ford
___HP551 *Healing Heart*, R. Druten
___HP552 *The Vicar's Daughter*, K. Comeaux
___HP555 *But for Grace*, T. V. Bateman
___HP556 *Red Hills Stranger*, M. G. Chapman
___HP559 *Banjo's New Song*, R. Dow
___HP560 *Heart Appearances*, P. Griffin
___HP563 *Redeemed Hearts*, C. M. Hake
___HP567 *Summer Dream*, M. H. Flinkman
___HP568 *Loveswept*, T. H. Murray
___HP571 *Bayou Fever*, K. Y'Barbo
___HP576 *Letters from the Enemy*, S. M. Warren
___HP579 *Grace*, L. Ford
___HP580 *Land of Promise*, C. Cox
___HP583 *Ramshackle Rose*, C. M. Hake
___HP584 *His Brother's Castoff*, L. N. Dooley
___HP587 *Lilly's Dream*, P. Darty
___HP588 *Torey's Prayer*, T. V. Bateman
___HP591 *Eliza*, M. Colvin
___HP592 *Refining Fire*, C. Cox
___HP599 *Double Deception*, L. Nelson Dooley
___HP600 *The Restoration*, C. M. Hake
___HP603 *A Whale of a Marriage*, D. Hunt
___HP604 *Irene*, L. Ford
___HP607 *Protecting Amy*, S. P. Davis
___HP608 *The Engagement*, K. Comeaux
___HP611 *Faithful Traitor*, J. Stengl
___HP612 *Michaela's Choice*, L. Harris
___HP615 *Gerda's Lawman*, L. N. Dooley
___HP616 *The Lady and the Cad*, T. H. Murray
___HP619 *Everlasting Hope*, T. V. Bateman
___HP620 *Basket of Secrets*, D. Hunt

___HP623 *A Place Called Home*, J. L. Barton
___HP624 *One Chance in a Million*, C. M. Hake
___HP627 *He Loves Me, He Loves Me Not*, R. Druten
___HP628 *Silent Heart*, B. Youree
___HP631 *Second Chance*, T. V. Bateman
___HP632 *Road to Forgiveness*, C. Cox
___HP635 *Hogtied*, L. A. Coleman
___HP636 *Renegade Husband*, D. Mills
___HP639 *Love's Denial*, T. H. Murray
___HP640 *Taking a Chance*, K. E. Hake
___HP643 *Escape to Sanctuary*, M. J. Conner
___HP644 *Making Amends*, J. L. Barton
___HP647 *Remember Me*, K. Comeaux
___HP648 *Last Chance*, C. M. Hake
___HP651 *Against the Tide*, R. Druten
___HP652 *A Love So Tender*, T. V. Batman
___HP655 *The Way Home*, M. Chapman
___HP656 *Pirate's Prize*, L. N. Dooley
___HP659 *Bayou Beginnings*, K. M. Y'Barbo
___HP660 *Hearts Twice Met*, F. Chrisman
___HP663 *Journeys*, T. H. Murray
___HP664 *Chance Adventure*, K. E. Hake
___HP667 *Sagebrush Christmas*, B. L. Etchison
___HP668 *Duel Love*, B. Youree
___HP671 *Sooner or Later*, V. McDonough
___HP672 *Chance of a Lifetime*, K. E. Hake
___HP675 *Bayou Secrets*, K. M. Y'Barbo
___HP676 *Beside Still Waters*, T. V. Bateman
___HP679 *Rose Kelly*, J. Spaeth
___HP680 *Rebecca's Heart*, L. Harris
___HP683 *A Gentlemen's Kiss*, K. Comeaux
___HP684 *Copper Sunrise*, C. Cox
___HP687 *The Ruse*, T. H. Murray
___HP688 *A Handful of Flowers*, C. M. Hake
___HP691 *Bayou Dreams*, K. M. Y'Barbo

(If ordering from this page, please remember to include it with the order form.)

Presents

Great Inspirational Romance at a Great Price!

Heartsong Presents books are inspirational romances in
contemporary and historical settings, designed to give you an
enjoyable, spirit-lifting reading experience. You can choose
wonderfully written titles from some of today's best authors like
Wanda E. Brunstetter, Mary Connealy, Susan Page Davis,
Cathy Marie Hake, Joyce Livingston, and many others.

When ordering quantities less than twelve, above titles are $2.97 each.
Not all titles may be available at time of order.

SEND TO: **Heartsong Presents** Readers' Service
          P.O. Box 721, Uhrichsville, Ohio 44683

Please send me the items checked above. I am enclosing $ _____
(please add $3.00 to cover postage per order. OH add 7% tax. WA
add 8.5%). Send check or money order, no cash or C.O.D.s, please.
          To place a credit card order, call 1-740-922-7280.

NAME _____

ADDRESS _____

CITY/STATE _____ ZIP_____

HEARTSONG
PRESENTS

If you love Christian romance…

$10.99

You'll love Heartsong Presents' inspiring and faith-filled romances by today's very best Christian authors…Wanda E. Brunstetter, Mary Connealy, Susan Page Davis, Cathy Marie Hake, and Joyce Livingston, to mention a few!

When you join Heartsong Presents, you'll enjoy four brand-new, mass market, 176-page books—two contemporary and two historical—that will build you up in your faith when you discover God's role in every relationship you read about!

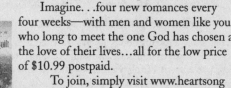

Mass Market 176 Pages

Imagine…four new romances every four weeks—with men and women like you who long to meet the one God has chosen as the love of their lives…all for the low price of $10.99 postpaid.

To join, simply visit www.heartsong presents.com or complete the coupon below and mail it to the address provided.